D0209373

The Gift

Books by T. Davis Bunn

The Gift
The Maestro
The Presence
Promises to Keep
The Quilt
Riders of the Pale Horse

The Priceless Collection

Secret Treasures of Eastern Europe

1. *Florian's Gate*
2. *The Amber Room*
3. *Winter Palace*

Rendezvous With Destiny

Rhineland Inheritance
Gibraltar Passage

The Gift

T. Davis Bunn

BETHANY HOUSE PUBLISHERS
MINNEAPOLIS, MINNESOTA 55438

Published by Bethany House Publishers
A Ministry of Bethany Fellowship, Inc.
11300 Hampshire Avenue South
Minneapolis, Minnesota 55438

Printed in the United States of America

Library of Congress Cataloging-in-Publication Data

Bunn, T. Davis, 1952–
    The gift / T. Davis Bunn.
       p.   cm.
    1. Hospital patients—Fiction. I. Title.
PS3552.U4718G54   1994
813'.54—dc20   94–25695
ISBN 1–55661–527–2   CIP

This book is dedicated to
My sisters in life and in Spirit,
Bunny Matthews and Nancy Smith.

And to their wonderful husbands,
Foxy and Justin.

"The Spirit and the bride say, 'Come!'
And let him who hears say, 'Come!'
Whoever is thirsty, let him come;
And whoever wishes, let him take
The free gift of the water of life."

REVELATION 22:17

IT WAS AS CLEAR to her now as the dawn sky. Clear and glorious in its stillness, like a lake she used to visit with her husband, surrounded by forests and hills, so deep in its valley that few breezes found their way down to mar the mirror-like surface. The two of them would walk down while morning was nothing more than a rosy hint above the eastern hills, holding hands like teenagers, stepping carefully along the stone path so they did not spill their brimming coffee mugs. The world was silent then, and theirs. They would sit at the end of the dock, hands intertwined and bodies touching, sipping coffee for warmth, watching the colors grow into day, hearing the woods

come alive, sharing what could never be put into words. It was one of the few times in her life when Grace could remember being happy and silent at the same time. Perhaps that was why she thought of it now. She was not by nature a quiet woman. Yet here and now there was simply no room for words.

Grace had few regrets about her life. A pinch of this, a dash of that, love and laughter in good measure, a few tears to soften her vision when what she saw was too much to bear. Faith in abundance, striving never to count the minutes spent in prayer and study, even when time was measured and squeezed and burdened. For Grace truly loved her God. It was a love rich in depth and full of flavor. She loved Him with fervor. She loved Him with gusto. And, most of all, she loved Him with honesty.

Grace also loved life. Sometimes she felt overwhelmed by the incredible richness of living. This feeling swept her up at the strangest times. One was the day of her husband's death. He fought his illness for nine long and harrowing months, battling with the same iron-hard strength that had powered him through life. He knew this was one struggle he could not win, yet he struggled just the same.

He managed to live long enough to hold his granddaughter. The little girl was born in the same hospital, two floors below where he lay. When he heard his daughter-in-law was entering labor, he ordered the doctors to take him off the painkillers. His voice was ravaged by the same ferocious beasts that tormented his body. Still he demanded it, this wasted husk of a man, who had spent every ounce of himself on the effort to see his first grandchild live and breathe and replace him upon the earth.

And he had won.

When the little girl was born, her mother spent a scarce moment marveling at this incredibly perfect miracle, then asked, is he still with us? The doctors had already called up, for all knew of the man's silent struggle, and replied with shared triumph, he is indeed. The newborn was bathed and fed and rushed to his bedside. The hospital's entire medical team stood and watched the drama unfold, honoring the man's final and greatest struggle with the gift of awe.

Grace herself held the infant up close to the destroyed face of her beloved husband, and with her own son watching from the foot of the bed, whispered to the newborn, "Behold, my child, behold the face of bravery."

Her husband managed to raise one hand. He stroked the child's soft little head, and whispered, "Her name?"

"Carmelita," John, their son, replied.

The old man nodded. It had been his own mother's name. "Tell her I was there to greet her," he said, each word a conquest.

"She will know you," Grace promised. "I will feed her with stories."

"It is good," he said, and died.

Later that day, Grace had left the hospital exultant with the glory of life. She was nothing if not a realist, and knew that soon enough the hollow aching loss would penetrate. But not now. The moment buoyed her up beyond the reach of her exhaustion and her heart's injury, sending her soaring like a balloon freed from a child's hand, bounding upwards in glorious communion with the sky and the clouds and with heaven.

Such times Grace considered to be her own special gift, and she did not talk about them. Instead, she tried to share the results. She tried to give the zest, the zing, to others, lifting them as she herself had been lifted, raising them beyond the mundane. The older generation tended to smile behind their hands and call her a firecracker. Younger ones called her a trip. But they loved her, and they came to her with their tears and their furies and their laughter and their triumphs.

And yet this time the gift was different. This time, laying here and watching the morning strengthen, there was no room for sharing, not now. It was all too intense.

The gift itself had come just before dawn's first light, a reward for the honesty with which she had addressed God and finally looked at herself. Now Grace lay in the stillness, listening to what was unheard. She was aware of freedom from the anger that had so marred her past three weeks, ever since her accident.

Grace was proficient in the cooking of many countries, and used food as bribe and lubricant and lever. Family gatherings were raucous, with everybody talking and Grace filling in the gaps with her own brand of humor. Empty places at the table were filled with neighbors and cousins and their childhood friends, now grown up to have children of their own. While the kids crawled about their feet or filled her home's now-empty spaces with their noise, Grace fed and talked and laughed and listened. Her listening had a piercing quality. She somehow managed to hear the unspoken.

But never had she heard with such clarity as she did now.

Grace kept a small leather-bound book with her Bible. It was as close to a diary as she had ever come. No page held more than a few sentences. Each entry marked what for Grace was a milestone in her growth. She only wrote in her diary when she felt she had reached the essence of something. She often went for weeks between entries.

The entries came in two forms. Working

from the first page onward, Grace wrote down truths she had discovered about herself. She often thought the blank page was the most honest mirror she had ever found.

Writing from the back page towards the front, Grace wrote down Scripture passages she felt she had drawn so deep inside herself that they had truly become a part of her.

Two blue ribbons kept her places. When the ribbons joined somewhere near the middle, Grace would retire that diary and start another.

Her last entry had been late the night before, after another battle with her son John. The pain in her hip had worsened with the resulting tension, and had finally stripped away the lie of her anger. After John had left, Grace had laid there in her lonely house, the darkness filled with the echoes of their raised voices, and realized her anger had only been a cloak for what she had refused to see.

Her entry that night had been just four short words:

I am so afraid.

John entered the house and walked directly to the kitchen. Elsie was there preparing Grace's breakfast tray. He asked, "Is she in her room?"

Elsie did not bother looking up. "Now where else is she gonna be this time of day? Any time, for that matter."

"Has she gotten up?"

"Made it as far as the bathroom," Elsie replied. "That's about it. Looks to me like her hip's complaining more than usual."

John inspected the strong dark face hovering over the stove. "Has she been giving you a hard time again?"

"She tries to now and again," Elsie replied, not giving it any more than that. "I don't pay her any mind."

"I don't know what we'd do without your help," John said solemnly.

"Don't you worry none," Elsie replied, understanding him perfectly. "I'm not about to let you down. Or her. No matter how short she tries to get with me."

John's birth certificate gave his name as Juan. But the six-year-old Juan had shown his father's stubbornness and insisted he be known by the English name. John it had remained ever since. "We argued again last night."

Elsie humphed. Sunlight through the kitchen window turned her dark skin the color of old mahogany. She had offered to help out in the mornings after Grace's accident, both as a favor to John and because she thought so much of Grace. Most of the time. "Sugar, tell me something I don't already know. The whole neighborhood's been listening in morning and night."

"I'm not a good arguer," John confessed.

"Most men aren't," Elsie announced with great satisfaction.

"Fights like those I've been having with Mama stay in me for days," John went on. "I haven't had a good night's sleep since her accident."

John was lean and hard like his father, and shared the same way of moving, silent and swift. He even spoke like the old man had, laying out each word with the careful deliberation of a bricklayer. His hair was jet black, his eyes hinted at an Indian's slant, and his skin was the color of a well-worn saddle.

Elsie handed him a cup of coffee without being asked. "I can't get over how you can drink that stuff first thing in the morning."

John took a cautious sip. It was just the way he liked it, heavily sugared and flavored with a good dollop of condensed milk. "Perfect."

"Tastes like a cup of coffee ice cream that's been left in the sun all day." Elsie replaced the can of treacly milk in the cabinet next to the refrigerator. She turned back to him, and cocked her head to one side. "Something I've been meaning to ask you, how's it you and your mama don't have any accent?"

There was too much friendship and too many debts to shrug off a question from Elsie. "My mother was raised in America."

"She told me the other day she was raised poor. Strange how she would say it like that, you know, instead of saying where she was from. I kinda took it her folks musta been wetbacks."

John took another swallow, and forced his

hand to remain steady. "Mama has some secrets all her own. She was an orphan, I know that much. She was raised by a family called Johnson."

Elsie clucked her concern. "White folks?"

"Yes, and they did not speak a word of Spanish," John went on, though it was hard. Very hard. But if anyone had earned the right to know as much of the truth as he did, it was Elsie. "Mama never would speak Spanish. Not with me, not with Pop, not ever. Most of the time Pop spoke to her in Spanish, and she'd talk back in English. Whenever he talked with her in English we knew he was in a good mood."

"Courtly," Elsie added. "That was the way your daddy spoke English. I'll always remember that, how he made me feel like it was an honor when he talked with me."

"Mama understands Spanish perfectly. I remember when I was growing up, the neighborhood kids who spoke Spanish used to say things we thought she wouldn't understand, and then we'd say something over the edge and she'd smack us good. But if somebody spoke to her in

Spanish, first she'd reply in English, and if they couldn't understand, she'd drag me over and make me translate."

"Sounds like a tragedy's been buried down deep," Elsie murmured.

John nodded, sipping at coffee he no longer tasted, and recalled, "There was a time when I was still a kid, Mama started having nightmares. Not often, but often enough. She would wake up the whole house, she was that loud. I remember she spoke in a voice that scared me because it wasn't hers. She sounded like a little girl. A very, very frightened little girl. And she spoke in Spanish."

"Lord, Lord, Lord," Elsie murmured, her voice a deep-throated chant.

"Pop would wake up, and speak back to her in Spanish," John went on, lost in his memories. "That was the only time I ever heard Mama talk with him in his own language. Those nights were hard on me."

Elsie reached over, took the coffee mug from his unfeeling fingers. "You best be getting on in there."

John released the memory with a tight shudder. "I spoke with the doctor this morning. He was supposed to leave for a conference tomorrow, but he's delaying his departure long enough to operate on Mama. She has to go in today. She has to."

"Brother, you're busy telling the wrong person. The body who needs those words is in the next room."

John looked at the kitchen wall separating them from his mother. "Has she had her coffee?"

"Over an hour ago." Elsie reached out strong hands, spun him around, and shooed him on. "Go on, now. I'll be in here praying hard as I know how."

For all his strength, John was not a fighter. Walking down the hallway and knocking on his mother's door took more effort than working ten hours on a winter site. He stopped and knocked and tried to ease the knot in his belly. When he heard her faint voice, it took two deep breaths to find the strength to turn the knob.

Grace was seated in her big four-poster bed, propped up as high as the accident would allow. The morning paper lay in a heap on the floor. Her Bible lay open on what had been Enrico's pillow. Her leather-bound diary was there beside it. John's own ledgers and account-books were spread in an arm's-length semicircle. Looking down at her, John had the fleeting sensation that the books and papers were intended as anchors to hold her there, help her resist doing what they both knew had to be done.

Three weeks earlier, Grace had slipped in the shower stall. Because she had flatly refused to so much as step foot in the clinic for x-rays, the doctor could only guess at the extent of the problem. He had poked and prodded and watched her try to keep the pain from her face, and decided it had to be a hairline fracture of her pelvic bone. Anything less and Grace would not have been trapped in bed for three full weeks. Not Grace. Anything more and the pain would have driven her into the hospital, which in John's mind might have been better than having to watch her waste away.

It hurt John more than he could say to see her this way. Grace was normally so *active*. She had always been a big woman. But since the accident Grace had become both smaller and shapeless. Now the flesh rested uncomfortably upon her frame, the skin flaccid and formless. Throughout the past three weeks, her gaze had held battle-flags. Every time he had entered the room, Grace's eyes had stared up at him with undisguised hostility. Even her greetings had sounded like war trumpets.

But this morning, the angry glint was gone.

His rehearsed arguments died on his lips. "What's wrong, Mama?"

"Good morning to you too," she replied, but without the sharp edge of previous visits. "Pull up that chair and sit down."

John stood where he was. "Are you feeling all right?"

Instead of replying, Grace turned her head and looked to the bedroom's tall bay window. Sunlight streamed through lace curtains and fell in a pillar so brilliant it appeared almost solid. "I've been thinking about your father."

The calmness of her voice, rather than the words, rendered John speechless.

"The window was his gift, did I ever tell you that?" She did not wait for his reply. "Our first ten years of marriage were very hard. Enrico used to say it was good we both held dreams of better days."

"I remember," John said, finding a faint shade of his voice. "He said that some months dining on dreams was the only thing that kept you two from starving."

"We three," she corrected. "You were born towards the end of that time. Enrico called your birth God's herald of better days to come."

"I remember that too," John said, reaching for a hard-backed chair. His movements were gradual, as soft as his voice, striving not to disturb the moment. Whatever the reason, he did not want this to end. "When I was three or four, I used to think I had two names. My inside name was Haraldo, and my outdoor name was Juan."

She looked at him over the wire-rimmed

spectacles. "You never told me that."

"I've got a few secrets of my own, Mama," he replied, and instantly regretted it.

But to his relief her tone did not sharpen. Instead she turned her head toward the side alcove. "I have always loved the sun," she said. "When Enrico started building our home, he told the architect to draw the plans around a bay window facing east and looking out over the garden. The first piece of furniture we bought for the home was that loveseat." She was silent a long time, then said, "How I loved the dawns we shared, watching the sun rise and planning the day together."

The pillar of light passed through the lace curtains and fell upon the rickety wooden bench, turning it into a throne of molten amber. The cushions his mother had sewn were so brilliant that they seemed to possess a light of their own. His father's Spanish Bible, resting upon his place as it had since his funeral, lost its battered appearance and was made new in the shimmering illumination.

John asked again, "How are you feeling, Mama?"

"My hip," she said softly. "It hurts me."

John felt panic grow at the sound of her voice. For a fleeting instant he could see her age, and he glimpsed a world without his mother. A knife twisted deep in his heart. "We have to go, Mama. Today. We have to. The doctor says it is not going to heal unless he operates and sets the bone. A hairline fracture is still serious, and he won't be sure that's all it is until you let him x-ray you."

The words were not new. He had been saying them every morning and evening since the accident. What was new was Grace's quiet tone. "How is Carmelita?"

"Mama, listen to what I am saying," John pleaded. His only child, Grace's granddaughter, had grown so distraught over their arguments that she was refusing to come with him anymore. "The doctor says it is a relatively simple procedure. But the longer you wait, the greater the risk. You aren't young anymore. Remaining with this condition weakens you."

Grace turned back toward her son, inspected him a moment, and said mildly, "Would you just look at your shirt."

John glanced down at the blue denim, saw nothing unusual. It was caked with dust from the job-site and with the salt of old sweat, same as every day. "Mama, this is important."

"You really should get married again," she said.

"Living in such pain keeps you from resting well," John persisted. "It is damaging your resistance."

She looked at him and smiled. It was the first smile John had seen from her in almost a month. "Such strength," she said. "Such goodness. Such love for a stubborn old woman. How have I ever come to deserve such a son?"

Weakness flooded in with relief. "Then you'll go?"

"Ask Elsie to come in," she replied. "I'll need to tell her what to pack."

Leslie Denton's first thought when her high-heel jammed in the outdoor escalator's top ledge was, I don't have time for this.

Then the escalator itself jammed, making a noise like a blender striking on a nail. A horn sounded somewhere, the stairs braked to a jarring halt, and the people crowded on behind her all fell forward in a heap.

She heard her ankle go from inside herself, a sound like chewing on ice, only a lot farther down.

Strangely enough, there wasn't much pain at first. More embarrassment over causing a scene, and anger at the fleshy man who lay panting and struggling on top of her, pressing the back of her new suit into a rain puddle. Leslie struggled to push him off, and said, "Do you *mind*?"

Then the grunting man was simply not on her anymore.

Leslie looked up at a lean, bronze-skinned man in a denim work shirt. Although not very big, he was obviously quite strong. She could tell that much by the way he easily propped up the vastly bigger man and quietly asked him, "Are you hurt?"

The man was having trouble bringing his morning into focus. "Uh, I don't know what happened, one minute I was—"

The lean man shook him gently, just hard enough to get his attention. Mexican probably, Leslie decided, although it was hard to tell. Strange that his English had no accent. Stranger still that her mind would focus on something like that at a time like this. She heard the bronze-skinned man say, "I have to help the lady. Can you stand on your own?"

"Sure, yeah, like I said—"

But the man had already turned away to right an older lady's shopping bag and help her rise to her feet. He asked if all was okay, his quiet voice somehow commanding immediate respect as he stood on the now silent escalator.

A grey-haired gentleman in a cashmere overcoat struggled unsteadily to his feet, caught his briefcase on the escalator stair, and would have gone down again on top of Leslie. But before she could even manage to gasp, the lean man was there to catch the older gentleman and *lift* him over Leslie.

"Oh, well, thank you," the startled gentleman said.

"Call 911," the worker said quietly. "Ask for an ambulance."

Clearly the gentleman was not used to receiving orders from a sweaty construction worker. "Look here—"

"Tell them to hurry," the man said, swinging about to face the man square on. "There's a telephone right over there. I need to help the lady. Will you do it?"

The gentleman glanced down at Leslie, and comprehension filtered through. "Yes, of course. Right away."

"Good." The man looked down at Leslie and said only, "You probably shouldn't move."

But she was already struggling to raise herself from the puddle. "My heel is still caught," she said, and managed to sit up. Then she saw the ridiculous angle of her shoe and her foot and her leg, and a queasiness struck her belly with the force of a fist. "My ankle. I think it's broken."

"I think so too," the man said, then turned back to the escalator. A young up-and-comer in a fancy Italian suit struggled by the old woman with the shopping bag, only to meet the man's straight arm right in his chest. "Turn around and go back down."

"But I'm late for an appointment," the young man complained.

"There's a woman trapped here. Go back down."

"You don't understand. I'm late for—"

Still holding the young man at bay, the construction worker raised his voice and called out, "Turn around!" Something in his voice caused the hustle-bustle nine o'clock morning crowd to pause. "Turn around! There's an injured lady trapped at the top! Go back down and use the stairs!"

The crowd stopped its forward push, grumbled at having their workaday routine interrupted, then slowly turned and clumped back down. The young man realized he wasn't getting through without a fight which he might well not win, and turned back, muttering under his voice. The worker grabbed for his arm and said, "Think maybe you could stop anybody else from starting up?"

"Yeah, right," the young man snorted, shrugged his arm free, and started down.

A pair of dark blue trousers appeared beside Leslie. "What's going on here?"

"The lady's trapped," the worker said, crouching down beside Leslie. His face was angular and leathery, but the coal-black eyes showed kindly concern. To the security guard he said, "It'd sure help if you could stop people from using the escalator until I get her free."

"No problem," the man said, stepping carefully over Leslie. "Old geezer told me to tell you the ambulance is on its way."

"Thanks."

Suddenly Leslie's teeth were chattering. "Can't you do something?"

"Yes," the man replied, reaching into his pocket. He came up with a well-worn Swiss army knife. He selected the smaller blade, which was honed to razor sharpness, and said, "Sorry about your shoe, but I can't risk twisting your foot any more." Then he sliced the polished leather from instep to toe, and made another slice at the heel.

"There goes my only pair of Guccis," Leslie said, trying not to look at the swiftly swelling ankle. The strange lumps under the skin only made her feel worse. But maybe it wasn't too bad—there still wasn't much pain. If only she didn't feel so cold. It had to be the puddle she was sitting in. "I hardly ever wear heels outside the office. But you know how it is. I was at a meeting with our lawyers in the building just behind us, and had to rush back to my office. I work for Draycon. What is it, two hundred yards? Who'd have thought something like this could happen, I mean, I must walk this patch a dozen times a week." Leslie realized she was jabbering, and doing so with a grimy construction worker she had never seen before in her life, and all the while the shivers were working their way down through her entire frame.

"Okay," the man said, peeling the entire side of her shoe down and away. "I'm going to slide my hand under your foot now, and ease it out. Don't you try to help me."

"I don't think I've even thanked you," Leslie said.

The man raised his head. "Did you hear what I said?"

"Of course." The shivers were coming so hard now she had difficulty getting the words out.

Concern knitted his brow. He raised one hand and touched her cheek, just as a siren howled up close and then growled into silence. The man looked over her shoulder at the sound of running feet and a voice saying, "What's up?"

"Broken ankle, by the looks of it," the construction worker said, his voice still calm. "Better get a couple of blankets. She's going into shock."

Shock. Leslie had heard of that, but never had any idea what it really was. She watched from a shivering mental distance as the lean man bent back down over her foot. She tried to ask, "What's your name?" But the shivers were so bad now the words were mangled into insensibility.

"Okay, I'm sliding my hand in." Gently his fingers probed down under the arch of her foot. "Don't even think of moving." His free hand gripped Leslie's leg just below the knee. Then together the two hands guided her entire lower leg to the side, a millimeter at a time, out of the shoe.

"That's great, hold it right like that," said a voice accompanied by running steps. A blanket was hastily draped about her trembling shoulders, then a white uniform bent down beside the worker. "Okay, hold it steady, I'm going to wrap this cold-pack around the ankle, yeah, that's it."

Rattling wheels announced the arrival of a stretcher. Leslie lifted her head, intending to thank the ambulance driver who was lowering the bed down to ground level, and realized she had drawn a crowd of curious onlookers.

But before embarrassment could set in, pain *slammed* through her. She drew breath to cry out, when a second lance shot up her leg and through her body and smashed her consciousness into a thousand pieces, and the world faded to blackness.

The first thing that filtered through the sleepy fog and reached her awareness was thirst.

The second was the smell. There was no mistaking the sharp, almost metallic tang in her mouth and nostrils. Anesthesia. Then she felt the crisp starchiness of sheets laundered to insensibility, and heard the strange sounds of loudspeakers and clanging beds and squeaky rubber-soled shoes in the corridor outside, and Leslie knew. She was in a hospital.

The ankle ached with a dull throb in time to her heartbeat. But the leg was immobile, and the pain had a sense of rightness to it. Strange that she would think of it in those terms, but that was how it felt. Leslie licked her dry lips, feeling relief because she had managed to sleep through the ordeal.

She opened her eyes. The room was painted

with hospital pastels, and was small enough to look cramped with its two beds. Her neighbor was old and Hispanic and appeared to be asleep. Leslie looked down at herself, saw how her ankle was wrapped in clean white bandages and encased in what appeared to be the bottom half of a plaster cast. Her left arm was attached to a drip. Leslie spotted a plastic drinking mug with straw on her bedside table, and fumbled for it, feeling as though she had never been so thirsty in her life.

As she sipped the ice-cold water, the door whooshed open to admit a black nurse wearing a stiff blue uniform and a brisk attitude. "Well, hello there," she said, flashing a swift nurse's smile and then tucking it back out of sight. She reached for Leslie's wrist and swung her watch into view. "How are you feeling?"

"Okay. Is this Providence General?"

"Sure is." The nurse slid a disposable thermometer under Leslie's tongue, counted the seconds, pulled it out, nodded once.

"How is my ankle?"

"You'll have to ask the doctor." She bustled

about, pulled up her records from their slot at the foot of her bed, made a note.

"Who treated me?"

"Doctor Collins. You met him downstairs on your way in."

"No I didn't."

The nurse smirked knowingly. "You don't remember anything about when they brought you in?"

"I've been out cold since the accident."

"Not the whole time, you haven't," the nurse replied, and turned the report around. "Isn't this your signature on the release form?"

Leslie squinted, and said, "It can't be." But it was.

"The doctor couldn't have operated without your consent." The nurse slipped the folder back in its slot and walked back around. "I'm going to raise your bed a little."

The anesthetic fog was gradually clearing away. Leslie found herself growing increasingly irritated with this nurse. Everything she said felt like a subtle put-down, as though she was intending to establish right off who was boss. "I'd rather lay down a while longer."

"It's important that you sit up to help your circulation," the nurse said, operating the electronic control. When the bed was cranked up, she slid one hand expertly behind Leslie, propped her forward, and plumped her pillow. "There. These buttons here operate your bed. This is for your television, and this for radio. The call button is here. Now is there anything else?"

"Yes." Leslie glanced at the woman beside her, who thankfully was still asleep. "My insurance specifically grants me a single room."

A hard glint appeared in her eyes as the nurse recognized a challenge. "Ma'am, this hospital happens to be full to the brim. The only reason you're not in the public ward with all our other emergency patients is because this woman was kind enough to share *her* private room with *you*." The nurse paused with evident satisfaction. "Now is that all?"

Leslie managed a nod, hoping desperately the woman in the other bed was truly asleep. When the nurse bustled off, Leslie sank down on her pillow and risked another glance at the other bed. Great, the eyes were still closed.

Leslie gave the sleeping woman a frank inspection. She was brown skinned and grey haired and flat faced, and about as shapely as a loaf of bread. Leslie turned back and heaved an internal sigh. Wonderful. Trapped in a hospital for who knew how long, sharing her room with a retired maid.

For Grace, the day was filled to bursting with stillness.

She lay propped up slightly, the hospital bedcovers drawn back and a day-blanket cast over her legs. She kept her eyes closed, both to keep from embarrassing the young woman next to her and to hold on to the serenity.

The gift had been given to her again that morning. The same, yet different.

The three days since her own operation had been the longest of her adult life, lying there immobile, alone even when her family had been gathered around her, afraid at the very time the nurses were assuring her the operation had gone extremely well. The doctor was attending a conference, they had told her time and again, as though she would feel better knowing the reason behind his absence. She had not cared. She had scarcely heard them. Since awakening from the operation she had been kept busy fighting off memories and boredom and the looming specter of a future spent growing old.

But now she had this.

The first time the gift had come, the morning before she had agreed to enter the hospital, Grace had been so startled as to have almost pushed its sensations away. This time she embraced them. She lay with eyes closed, knowing that soon the feelings would fade, that soon she would have to face her fears and the world and this woman lying next to her. Yet she also knew the gift's essence would somehow remain, as much a part of her now as the pain stabbing her hip.

And this knowing gave her strength.

It had all started with a lesson in her Bible study class almost a year earlier, during a discussion of visions in the Scriptures. The teacher had spoken of an ancient church father, who had taught his own students to picture a favorite Gospel scene in one's mind: Jesus at the well, teaching the multitudes upon the mount, confronting the temple Pharisees, walking upon the waters, calming the storm. The key, the teacher had said, was not to use one's imagination well, but to *listen* well. This had baffled most of the women, and they had covered their confusion with laughter. That would take all the fun out of prayer, one woman had said, I have too many problems I need to talk with God about to ever want to listen.

But Grace had not joined in the merriment. The lesson and the comments had struck too close to home. She had the ability to listen well, she knew that for a fact. But she had never really tried to listen to God. When she prayed, she talked. When she stopped talking, she stopped praying. It had never occurred to her before that she should try listening in prayer.

For some reason, the concept had frightened her.

Despite her misgivings, Grace had begun that very night. She had found the exercise extremely trying. Her mind would flitter from one point to the next, never slowing, never focusing, never holding still. Several times Grace almost gave up. But something had kept her going.

After several months, it had become a natural part of her twice-daily prayer time. She would start with her prayers, and when they were done, she would try to picture a Biblical scene. Because of where she had been in her own studies, she had chosen to concentrate upon the Crucifixion. She imagined herself seeing it or even being a part of the scene from many different perspectives; standing with the crowd, helping to carry the cross, watching the nails being driven in, looking up and trying to see His face. Occasionally the mental image held for a few moments, long enough for her to begin understanding the need to listen. It had not been words she had heard, but rather a tiny hint of silence. Of peace. Of something that remained beyond her normal, daily routine.

She had often been tempted to change and

think on something else, but she had resisted the urge. She felt sure her difficulties would not ease by concentrating on a different scene. Grace had also been worried that if she changed once, her mind would begin to switch faster and faster until the scenes became those of her own life, drawing her normal busy activity into these quiet moments.

Grace was too lively for such quietly focused thought to come easily. But she was also a determined woman and, over the days and weeks that followed, she became increasingly convinced that what she was trying to do was important. So important, in fact, that not even the accident halted her attempts.

And quiet she had become.

The morning before she had entered the hospital, prayer had been a painful experience. Her heart had been so heavy, filled with regret and shame for the anger she had shown her son, laden with fears she had carried all her life. In prayer her thoughts had remained so burdened that the words were slow in coming. Grace had then offered up her heart, her prayer transformed into a silent plea, ashamed and afraid, awash in memories.

Afterwards, when she had tried to picture the Crucifixion, the quiet had entered more strongly than ever before.

Like a rising tide, the stillness had simply enveloped her. Grace had felt it emanate both about her and within her heart. And in that moment she had understood what it meant to listen. To *hear*.

For three days afterwards, she had eagerly awaited a return to this wellspring of peace. Virtually every time she closed her eyes, she had tried to recapture the cross and the peace. Her disappointment had added hours to the lengthy days of laying on her hospital bed.

Finally, this very morning, understanding had dawned.

Grace lay with eyes closed and recognized she was attempting to do exactly what she had always done with prayer. She was telling God to give it to her. She was trying to direct what she received, and how it came. She was not listening. She was fueling her active mind with expectations.

And with this realization came a relaxing. An opening. A giving in. In this brief instant of peaceful waiting, she offered to the Lord her whole heart, and she asked Him to free her mind of any thought or desire or expectation not centered on *Him*.

And the Lord entered in.

This time the tide of peace contained a crystal clarity. Although the moment of truth retained its clearness for only an instant, the brief flash of insight contained a myriad of lessons. These insights were all things that she had known as a part of her faith for years and years, yet were somehow fresh and new here, seen in a unique and different way. A message given without words.

She was on a lonely hillside of rock and shale and sorrow, and looked up into a dark and gloomy sky. Great banks of clouds swept across the heavens, obliterating all light, all hope. The sun thrust a final ray through the thundering darkness, and it fell upon the central of three crosses.

The figure nailed there was a mere shadow of defeat and death. And yet, and yet, while she viewed this ultimate of defeats, she was *filled* with peace.

The scene faded from her mind's eye, but the peace remained. It rested upon her heart with a gentle caress. It spoke to her more clearly than any words could. Here is comfort. Here is hope. Here is life.

In the final fading moment, a voice which was no more than the smallest, quietest thought rose and spoke into her mind and heart. It said just one word:

Come.

FINALLY.

Waiting for the old woman to open her eyes had been misery. Leslie had never felt so trapped.

Her entire life had been spent building up the size of her world. Bigger office, bigger salary, bigger car, bigger status, bigger powers, bigger responsibilities. She had fought tooth and nail for a larger travel budget, then used every penny. She gobbled up newspapers and magazines, striving to keep the bigger picture always in focus.

Suddenly her world had been shrunk to a room measuring ten by twelve.

Everything she saw and smelled and felt and tasted was diminished. Her wristwatch was nowhere to be seen, probably stashed in the closet with her clothes. Which was a world away, as far as she was concerned. There was no clock in the room. While she had waited for the old woman to wake up, Leslie had been reduced to measuring the minutes by watching the sun's passage across the floor.

Being forced to wait while the old woman slept had been infuriating. Leslie had found herself growing increasingly enraged over the woman's presence. Never mind that it had originally been her room. Never mind that she was old and probably needed her rest. None of that mattered. Laying there trapped in a hospital bed, totally unable to move or work or even use the phone, Leslie grew angrier and angrier at the only person in sight—the old woman who refused to wake up.

The instant the woman finally sighed gently and opened her eyes, Leslie grabbed for the phone. She heard rather than saw the woman turn her head in Leslie's direction, but she was too angry just then to acknowledge her.

The first call was to her mother. They had

what Leslie considered to be a comfortable relationship. Her mother never did understand
why she had wanted to leave home. But they
had long since made peace over Leslie's direction. She in turn never forgot a birthday. She
went home for Thanksgiving and Christmas.
She called every Saturday after the rates went
down. Leslie Denton worked at being a good
daughter.

For some reason, her anger increased with
each ring of the phone, an unfocused, unchan-
neled frustration over the entire situation. When
her mother finally answered Leslie was unable
to really hear anything her mother said. Not that
it mattered. All their conversations followed a
fairly set pattern.

"Hi, Mom. Yeah, it's me. Nothing to worry
about, but I thought I'd let you know. I'm stuck
here at Providence General with a twisted ankle." She looked down at her leg while the
phone chattered back. "Can you believe it, of all
the stupid things, I get my heel caught in the
escalator. The one time I go outside not wearing
my Nikes. So ridiculous."

She waited through another little twitter of words from the handset, then went on, "Like my boss says around vacation time, if you're going to get hurt, at least be doing something either glamorous or where you can sue somebody. So hey, this could have been skiing in St. Moritz, but no, I've got to do it on the outdoor escalator coming back from our lawyers."

The phone chattered into her ear. Incredible that she could catch the meaning without really hearing the words. "No, I don't know how long. The doctor hasn't come by yet. I'll call you when I know anything more. Yeah, me too. Okay, Mom. Bye."

Call number two was to her office and basically followed the same pattern as the one to her mother, except she ended by asking them to messenger over anything urgent. Trying to put a little more humor into this one, let them know she was still on top of things, even though she was flat on her back.

Leslie hung up the phone and set it on the bedside table. She lay back, suddenly very tired.

"You need to take it easy today," the old

woman said, speaking for the first time. "Any operation really takes it out of you."

"I'm fine," Leslie replied, yet found herself without the strength to lift her head from the pillow. She then recalled that the woman had been willing to share her private room, and decided a little polite chit-chat was in order. Without looking over, she said, "My name is Leslie Denton."

"Hello, Leslie. I am Grace Mendez."

"Nice to meet you. What are you in for?" It sounded like two inmates talking in prison.

The bed beside her rustled. "Some name," the woman sighed.

"Excuse me?"

"Have you ever noticed," the woman said, "that the first thing a doctor does to a problem is attach a name? My husband had a name for his disease I have spent years trying to forget. The last time I was in a hospital was the day he died from it."

Her fatigue gradually eased a trifle. Leslie turned enough so she could see the woman in the next bed. It was strange to hear such clear, unaccented English coming from such a darkly Hispanic face. "I guess they have to label a problem before they can treat it."

The woman nodded her grave agreement, her eyes on the opposite wall. "That is certainly part of it. But I think for many doctors, the naming of a condition helps them keep it at arm's length. They do their inspections, and they assign a name. Then they can say, oh yes, this and this problem requires this and this treatment. They are safe. They are protected by their papers and their instruments and their machines. They do not need to *feel*. They do not have to say, here is a person in pain. A person who is frightened."

Leslie nodded her agreement and found herself confessing, "And angry."

"And helpless and trapped in her bed." The woman looked in Leslie's direction for the first time. Dark eyes examined her as she asked, "Are you angry?"

"Furious."

"I used up all my anger trying to stay out of here."

"And frustrated," Leslie added.

"Yes, a busy young woman like you, I can well imagine."

"I broke my ankle, I guess you heard that from the telephone conversations."

"Oh, I already knew," the woman replied. "My son was the one who helped free you. That is how I heard about your being admitted and could offer you this room."

Leslie was flooded with shame. Her son, of course, her son. And Leslie could not even remember the woman's name. To be honest, she had not even heard the introduction. What if she had heard Leslie speaking to the nurse? No, no, that did not even bear thinking about.

Leslie was saved from dredging up a suitable reply by the doctor bustling in. "Good afternoon, good afternoon. The two people I need to speak with right here together. Excellent. Saves me a trip up and down the corridors." He gave Leslie a professional smile. "How are you feeling now?"

Leslie's brow furrowed. The short balding man looked vaguely familiar. "Have I spoken to you before?"

The doctor thought that was quite funny. "You were a little out of it at the time, but yes, we did speak. I'm Dr. Collins. I operated on your ankle."

"How is it?"

"All in good time, my dear." He turned to the other bed. "And how are you this afternoon, Grace?"

The woman's name was Grace. Leslie felt relief at not having to ask her again.

"Improving," Grace replied.

"Glad to hear it. Sorry I had to run off immediately after your operation, but it was because your son was so insistent that I delayed my departure long enough to see to your hip."

"John was afraid if you waited I would change my mind," Grace told him. "And rightly so."

He gave a polite ha-ha. "Let's have a look at the incision. Can you roll over for me, please?" The doctor helped her with practiced motions, ignoring her grimace of pain. He swept up her nightshift, lifted one edge of the bandage, said, "Excellent, excellent. All right, you can settle back now. Have you been getting out of bed?"

"Yesterday and today. It hurts."

"Have the nurse give you something for the pain. Becoming mobile as quickly as possible is an important part of the healing process. The key is not to allow yourself to become overly weak." His tone became more aloof. "You had exactly what we thought, a fractured neck of femur, or thigh bone. This can come in a whole range of degrees, all of which require an operation. I am happy to tell you that although your bone cracked, the two parts did not separate. This meant you could walk on it as you did. Every time you put weight on it, however, the two parts impinged on one another, causing you pain. In your case the head of the femur did not lose its blood supply and atrophy, what we call avascular necrosis. We simply inserted three long screws to secure it back into place."

"So I should feel fortunate," Grace said.

"Indeed you should. You are already moving about, and hopefully you will be returning home at the end of the week. I think we should plan for Sunday." He gave another quick smile and turned around. "Most likely the same day for you, Miss Denton."

"I have to stay here a week?"

"Afraid so," he replied briskly, walking over and inspecting her cast. He straightened and gave her another of his professional smiles. "You have the most common form of fracture, for which you should be most grateful."

"Thanks ever so much."

"Believe you me, some of the other ankle fractures can be horrific. Considering what happened, with you falling both around and forward as you did, you got off easy." The doctor pointed to her bandage. "Yours is called an inversion injury. You tore the main ligaments only a bit here and here, they are generally stronger than bone. Mostly they were just stretched and should heal with time. But you did tear off bits of bone connected to the ligament. The lateral malleolus and the posterior malleolus were both broken. This is called a bi-malleoli fracture. Again, you were lucky, since the bone fragments did not pop through the skin as often happens. Nor did you have a Potts fracture of all three."

"Hooray, hooray," Leslie murmured, queasy from the doctor's description.

"We have manipulated the bones back into place and screwed in one plate. We'll probably want to take that out at some point." He patted the hard undercast supporting her ankle. "We've done a half-cast, what we call a back slab. When the swelling has lessened in a couple of days we will form the full cast." He smiled triumphantly. "Barring any unforseen development, we'll have you out of here and back on the streets this coming weekend."

"Thank you," Leslie managed weakly.

"Don't mention it." The doctor moved for the door. "Well, as you can imagine, I have quite a bit to see to after two days away. I'll be in to see you both again tomorrow."

When the door had sighed shut behind him, Grace said, "See what I mean?"

"I'm not a person to him," Leslie agreed tiredly. "I'm the ankle in 4-C."

It would be so easy to dislike this young lady.

She was everything Grace objected to in a so-called modern woman—pushy and arrogant and superficial. She built her world around what Grace thought of as teflon-coated relationships, sliding away at the first sign of trouble. She probably had no sense of family. Grace had listened as she spoke to her boss with exactly the same tone of voice she used with her mother. There was no telling what sense of morals she had. If any.

But Grace found herself treasuring the gift too much to let her natural reactions drive it away.

Although the divine moment had long since faded, still there remained a hint of peace, as mild and as beautiful as the scent from her son's flowers. Grace knew if she gave in to the temptation to remain distant and judgmental, this too would slip away.

Grace felt good about how the conversation with Leslie had gone, to a point. Beneath the polite surface was a shell as hard as stone, Grace knew, there to protect this Leslie Denton from ever showing her deeper emotions to the world. Grace glanced over, realized the young woman had slipped into sleep. She did the only thing she knew to do in such a situation, faced with a woman who was utterly alien from herself. She prayed.

She was still at it an hour later, feeling no closer to an understanding, when Leslie opened her eyes. As Leslie turned a sleep-blurred face toward the other bed, Grace gave her a warm smile. "Feeling better?"

Leslie offered a smile in return, one which for some reason twisted Grace's heart. There was so much of a sad little girl in that sleepy, unprotected face. Leslie asked, "How long have I been asleep?"

"An hour and a bit. Just what you should be doing, too."

At that moment, the door cracked open and a dark-haired elf with eyes like glittering agate poked in as quietly as she could. Which was not very quiet at all. "Oh good, you're not asleep."

"I'm also not alone," Grace admonished.

The little girl paid the other bed no mind.

She struggled to push the door open to its absolute maximum. Finally satisfied that the portal was well and truly subdued, she entered and half-walked, half-skipped to Grace's bed. "Daddy said he had something 'portant. He'll be back in thirty minutes to fetch me. He said if you were resting I had to wait out in the hall. Are you resting?"

Grace turned to Leslie and said in apology, "My granddaughter now has the run of the entire hospital. Shall I send her out?"

"It's fine, really," Leslie said, and appeared to mean the words.

"Look at what I did at school today," the little girl exclaimed. She lifted a crumpled page of cardboard which appeared to be attached to her hand with bright orange glue. "It's a string painting! See, I put a piece of string in a pot of paint, then I put it on the paper and fold the paper and pull it out."

"That's some painting," Grace observed. "May I introduce my granddaughter, Carmelita. She is usually known as Lita, a name which I am not sure I like."

The Gift

"Look, see, the teacher gave me a gold star. It's lots of fun. The teacher let us do lots and lots of strings."

"This is Miss Denton," Grace said to the dancing sprite. "Can you say good afternoon?"

"'Noon," she said, not turning around. "Look, Gramma, see, there's red and blue and yellow and gold."

Grace rolled her eyes in apology. "Very nice, dear."

"Excuse me," Leslie said. "Do you think she might be able to hand me my briefcase?"

"Of course," Grace replied, pulling tissues from her box and wiping the worst of the goo off the little girl's hands. "Can you be a good girl and hand Miss Denton her case?"

"I'm a good girl almost always," Carmelita replied, nodding her head in a great swinging arch. "Daddy says it's my nature."

"I would imagine they put it in the closet," Leslie said. "At least, I hope they did."

Proud of her importance, Carmelita marched over, opened up the closet door, and said, "Oooh, that's nice. Is that yours?"

"Yes. It's a little heavy."

"That's okay, I'm a big girl." Carmelita used both hands to pull out a sleek crocodile and burnished leather case with gold-plated latches. "How come you have something so nice?"

"The correct way to ask," Grace said, "is, what is your profession?"

"I am Assistant Vice-President at Draycon," Leslie replied crisply, accepting the case. "We're in the big steel and dark-glass building downtown."

"I know that one," Carmelita said excitedly. "My daddy is working there."

"Your father came to my rescue this morning," Leslie said, popping the locks and opening the case.

"I know that too, he told me when he picked me up from school." Carmelita stood on tiptoes and craned to see inside. She pointed and asked, "What is that?"

"This? It's my mobile telephone."

"Ah," Grace said. "And now my granddaughter is interested."

"You take it with you everywhere you go?"

"That's the idea."

"A proper young lady," Grace observed, "does not give more importance to possessions than she does to people."

Something about those words clearly rocked the young woman in the next bed. She faltered a moment, started to look in Grace's direction, but was pulled back by Carmelita asking, "You mean people can call you anywhere you go? What if you don't want to talk to anybody? Don't you ever want to be alone?"

The question appeared to hit her like a second blow, shaking her composure. Grace watched as Leslie struggled to find a reply. "It saves me a lot of time."

"What do you do with all that time, then?"

"It makes my work easier," Leslie amended.

"Oh, I see," Carmelita said, nodding vigorously. "Then you have more time to play."

Grace offered, "She will drown you in questions if you let her."

"Why isn't it plugged into the wall like Daddy's phone?"

"It has a built-in antenna and power supply,"

Leslie replied distractedly, her mind apparently held by the earlier words.

"But how can the phone number find you if you keep moving around?"

"Your daddy has a beeper, remember?" Grace reminded her. "It can find him too, if he wears it."

"Uh-huh," Carmelita said, clearly not impressed. "How do you hang up?"

"You press that little button there," Leslie replied. She paused in thought and then looked over and asked, "Your son wears a pager?"

"He should. He detests the thing and almost always leaves it either in the car or at home."

Carmelita gave one number an experimental tap and exclaimed, "Listen, it beeps like a real phone. Can you play 'Mary Had a Little Lamb' on it? I can."

Leslie asked, "What does your son need a pager for?"

"That's exactly what he says," Grace agreed, wondering what it was affecting the young woman.

"Can I call my daddy on it? No, he's in the

car. Wait, I know. Can I call my best friend Janice?"

"Not now, dear," Grace said. "Come over here and stop bothering the young lady."

"I'm not bothering you, am I." It was not a question.

"Come over here, Carmelita."

Reluctantly she walked over and allowed her grandmother to encircle her with one arm. Still, she kept her face turned towards Leslie. "What is your favorite toy?"

"Adults don't have toys like children do," Grace explained.

"Daddy does," Carmelita replied. "Daddy says I'm his favorite toy in the whole world, so favorite he doesn't have time for any other toy but me." She turned her attention back to Leslie. "What do you do for fun?"

"Well," Leslie had to stop and think about that one. "I like to ski."

"Where do you ski?"

"I try to get to Utah for a week every year."

"Just one week? Why do you only play one week a year? Don't you have the phone so people can call you everywhere and save you time so you can go out and play?"

"I'm very busy with my work," Leslie replied weakly, the briefcase laying open and forgotten on her bedside table.

"Daddy is very busy too. But he plays. He plays every day with me. He says playing with me is what keeps him young."

The door opened to admit a tall dark woman who exclaimed, "Girl, what was it your daddy told you to do?"

"I'm not bothering anybody, I'm not. Tell her I'm not, Gramma."

Elsie smiled down at Grace. "How you doing, honey?"

"Better," Grace replied, and smiled back.

"Now would you just look at that," Elsie said, walking over and taking Grace's hand. "A smile. If that isn't a sight for sore eyes."

Grace pressed the smooth-rough fingers. "You've always been able to bring that out in me."

"Not the past few weeks, I haven't." But the hand squeezed back. "What were you going on like that for, giving everybody such a hard time?"

"I was afraid," Grace said simply, for some reason not now ashamed in the least to admit it. She turned to her side and said, "May I introduce Leslie Denton. Leslie, this is my good friend Elsie Silver."

"Nice to meet you," the young woman replied in a subdued voice.

The smile turned towards the other bed. "I hear you gave John a run for his money. How's the leg?"

"Okay, thanks to her son."

"Yeah, John's a good boy." Elsie turned back to Grace. "Listen, honey. The next time you decide to get scared like that, I want you to let me know well in advance. I think I'll take me a vacation in Hawaii."

"I know where that is," Carmelita piped up. "It's an island but it's a state too. They wear lots of flowers."

"I hope it never happens again," Grace said. "Not ever."

"You and me both," Elsie agreed. The look

in her eyes let Grace know that the anger and the weeks of harsh words were well and truly behind them. She looked down at Carmelita and asked, "Have you been behaving yourself, missie?"

"Yes I have, ma'am, Miss Elsie. Haven't I, Gramma."

"She's been good," Grace agreed. "Loud, but good."

"I'm not loud," Carmelita objected. "Just engetic."

"Energetic," Elsie corrected fondly.

"Yeah, that's what daddy says. Engetic."

"You got the engetics of a tornado," Elsie agreed, rising to her feet. "Her daddy's tied up. Again. Asked me to come fetch her before she got to be a bother." She patted Grace's shoulder, snagged the little girl's hand and started for the door. "You be good now, hear? Nice to meet you, Leslie. Hope that leg heals up good and fast. Say 'bye to the nice ladies, Lita. We'll stop by again tomorrow."

John did not make it to the hospital until well after dark. He arrived tired and dusty and a little ashamed that work had kept him so busy for so long. He opened the door to Grace's room as softly as possible, stepped inside, and saw both women were asleep. He started to leave, but something held him. A streetlight outside their window cast a soft yellow glow over the room. Grace's face was set in gentle repose, her features relaxed into the slackness of age and illness. John looked down at his mother, and felt a tug at his heart.

Again he started to leave, and again he lingered. Feeling awkward, he looked down on the woman in the other bed. She was quite pretty in a brittle sort of way. The burden of time and cares were clearly seen. Faint feather strokes of grey touched her hair, for some reason more clearly visible in the poor light. John guessed her age at somewhere in the mid- to late thirties. She looked tired. Not just from the injury either. Lines of banked-up fatigue were etched across her forehead and tightened the sides of her eyelids even in sleep. He turned and slipped from the room.

"Ah good, just the man I wanted to see." The voice startled John, as though he had been caught doing something wrong. He turned to see Dr. Collins bustling towards him. "Is your mother asleep?"

"Yes."

"Right. I need to speak with you alone. Come over here and sit down for a moment." He led John to a side bench, waited until the weary man was seated, then asked, "How has your mother appeared to you since the operation?"

"All right, I guess," John replied, trying not to grow alarmed. "A little quieter than usual. No, make that a lot quieter."

"That's not a good sign, I'm afraid." The doctor's habitual briskness did not mask his gravity. "She may be losing interest in life. It happens with many older people who undergo such operations."

"It does?"

The doctor eyed him straight on. "I feel I should warn you that fifty percent of all older patients who undergo this surgery are dead within six months."

John felt his heart become encased in a solid block of ice. "What?"

"Not from the operation itself, mind you. But surgical trauma at their advanced age seems to sap their will to live. To put it simply, many of them lay down and simply decide not to get up. There appear to be two keys to success. The first is to immediately get them up and walking about. The second is to keep them interested in life. How old is your mother?"

It took him a moment to form the words. "Sixty-eight."

"Well, that's still relatively young. What interests her most? Or did, anyway, before she had the accident."

John struggled to focus. "Work and family." He tried to clear away the lump that had suddenly formed in his throat. "And cooking. And faith."

"She's a religious woman. Good. Studies show that tends to improve the survival rate." The doctor glanced at his watch and bounded to his feet. "My advice to you is to try and help her realize she is still needed. Now if you'll excuse me, I'm due in theater. Good evening."

John had to sit a very long time, isolated from the quietly bustling hospital activity by his shock and his sorrow, before his legs managed to carry him up and away.

Leslie drifted up out of sleep, drawn by a sense of recent movement in the room. The first thing she noticed was a faint smell of sweat. She turned her head, saw Grace was awake and staring at the ceiling, and asked, "Has somebody been in here?"

"My son," Grace replied. "He is about as subtle as his daughter."

"Oh. I'm sorry I missed him. I want to thank him for what he did."

"There will be time for that." Grace turned to look at Leslie. "Might I ask a favor of you?"

"Of course."

She motioned to a little book on the side table. "Would you do me the kindness of reading to me? My eyes, when I'm tired, you understand."

"Certainly." Leslie switched on her little overhead light, picked up the small leather-bound volume, and asked, "You keep a diary?"

"Not really. In the front I write a few thoughts when they occur to me. In the back I put down favorite Bible verses. I like to read a verse before retiring, when my eyes let me. It gives me something nice to think about in the night." She motioned with one hand, her dark gaze luminous in the soft light. "Just open it to wherever the second ribbon is, would you?"

Leslie did as she was told, and read, "Psalm 32, verse 3. 'In spite of His wonders, they did not believe. So He ended their days in futility.' "

"That is a nice one," Grace murmured sleepily, turning back towards the ceiling and closing her eyes. "In spite of His wonders, how often I do not believe. I worry if He will see me through this time, or relieve me of my fears, or help me face whatever is to come. And then that day ends with a sense of frustration and futility, no matter what I think I have accomplished. Thank you, my dear. I will sleep better now. Good night."

"Good night," Leslie said, turning off her light and laying back.

But the thoughts that whirled through her mind kept her from sleeping for quite a long time.

BY THURSDAY AFternoon, Leslie Denton felt her entire world was unraveling.

A massive bouquet of lilies and yellow roses crowded up against three smaller bunches. The large bouquet, which drew gasps from the most hardened of nurses, had been sent by her company. The smaller ones were from her mom and her department staff. The wall opposite her bed was now a fragrant jungle.

Yet Leslie had never felt so utterly isolated and alone in her entire life.

The only people who had visited her had been messengers collecting urgent documents. She had watched her briefcase's contents gradually dwindle, and known a sense of panic when nothing else arrived to take its place. Three times she had called her boss, insisting she was well enough to work. Each time she had been told they would call her as soon as she was up and about; but for the moment, her first duty was to heal. That morning Leslie had again listened to the bland words and the fake concern, and knew with utter certainty she had been taken out of the loop. When she hung up the phone, she vowed she would not tolerate such a humiliation again. Calls to the company would wait until she was back on her feet.

But she was not mending as fast as she should.

The swelling in her ankle was not subsiding. The full cast had still not been put into place. Leslie checked her watch for the fifth time in thirty minutes, raised it to her ear to see if it was still ticking. Another two hours until the doctor began his rounds.

The day had already held a series of aftershocks, little tremors that had left her feeling internally unstable and out of kilter. That morning, a group of ladies from Grace's Bible study had gathered in a seated circle about her bed, and prayed for her healing. Leslie had tolerated the whole thing as politely as she knew how, trying to focus on the work in her hands, when she heard Grace begin praying for *her*. Suddenly a flood of indescribable emotion welled up from somewhere deep within her, and it had been all Leslie could do to keep from crying.

Then there had been the daily phone call with her mom. Without warning, Leslie had found herself listening to their conversation from a distance, and hearing it as though for the very first time.

They were very well informed about the activities of each others' lives, she and her mother, but knew nothing of the emotions *behind* each others' actions. This gave them a false sense of closeness, she realized, and a surface harmony. She did not laugh very much or cry very much with her mother, Leslie had then seen, because they never allowed their feelings to show. Leslie had listened to herself tell her mom about the ankle, and realized that in truth her mom was not asking out of deep concern. Her mother made Leslie's life her own by talking about it with her bridge circle. Being well informed was a substitute both of them used for genuine intimacy.

After hanging up, Leslie had sat in her bed and plunged into the uncharted depths of internal honesty.

She hated the falseness of her mother's cheery demeanor and always had. Yet this day, this moment, Leslie could not escape from the fact that she had adopted her own brand of superficiality. Oh, she had done so for all the right reasons. Living life in the fast lane meant holding back, not allowing any attachments or commitments to slow her down. But it had also meant tainting every relationship she built, friends and lovers and family alike, with an uncaring legacy.

To make matters worse, the little granddaughter had bounded in just after lunch, full of life and joy and love for her gramma. Leslie had pretended to concentrate on a newspaper and listened to the two chatter until Carmelita had suddenly turned her way and asked, "Who do you love?"

"It is proper for little ladies to greet a person with their name," Grace had gently chided. "Before raining questions down on them."

Carmelita had shown a child's unabashed shyness as she turned back to her grandmother and confessed in a stage whisper, "I forgot her name."

"She is Miss Leslie."

"Oh yeah, I remember now. That's a pretty name." She spun back around. "Hi, Miss Leslie. Who do you love?"

The exchange had given Leslie a chance to recover from the query's simple power. "Lots of people," she hedged.

"Me too." She skipped around to the window, chanting the words. "I love Gramma and Daddy the most. Then I love Janice, she's my best friend in the whole world. And I love my dolls, especially Agnes, she's my favorite. And I love my teacher Miss Carroll. And I love lots of other people, but I forget who right now."

Leslie found herself hungering to be in-

cluded in the circle of love from this little girl.
"Would you like to have a flower?"

Carmelita bounded over. "Oh, can I?"

"You have just made a friend for life," Grace
said.

"I have far too many," Leslie replied, and
was again touched by the same gentle warmth
as had flooded her during the morning prayer.
"Why don't you choose a bunch and take them
home?"

Lita's eyes rounded into great dark moons.
"A whole bunch?"

"Be sure to take some of every kind," Leslie
said.

"What do you tell nice Miss Leslie," Grace
said.

"Oh thank you, thank you, I love flowers."
She raced up and flung her arms as far up and
around Leslie's neck as she could manage. "Can
I really choose some of each kind?"

"Take as many as you like," Leslie replied,
and for the second time that day found herself
struggling not to cry.

After Elsie had come to collect the child,

Grace went off for her daily walk down the hall. Leslie was left alone to ponder how such little things as a couple of phone calls and a little girl's joy could leave her feeling as though the world had been tilted on its axis.

A knock on the door brought her back. It opened to admit John, dusty and sweat-stained as usual. "Hi. Is it okay to come in?"

"Hello. Sure." Yesterday and the day before she had tried twice to thank him for his help. He had responded with polite detachment, as though he had done nothing more for her than give the time of day. Both visits he had entered and greeted her and politely asked about her injury. Then his attention had focused upon his mother. After that, she might as well have been in another room. Leslie had decided he was both aloof and not particularly interesting.

But this afternoon she was enormously glad to have anyone or anything break the flow of her thoughts. "Grace has gone down the hall. The doctor says she has to walk, and she prefers to use the shower near the nurse's station. It has a lower ledge for her to step over and metal rails she can hold on to."

John motioned towards the door. "Maybe I'd better wait outside and let you rest."

"Not at all. Please, pull up a chair."

"Okay, thanks." John was dark and muscular, and did not appear to have an ounce of extra fat on his entire frame. "I tried to make it earlier today so I wouldn't catch her asleep, and I still miss her."

"She won't be long."

"How's the ankle?"

Leslie started to reply with the standard line, but the scalding honesty of her inward inspection left her needing to tell someone the truth. "The swelling's not going down. It's really worrying me."

Sharp-edged, intelligent features turned to inspect her leg. "Does it hurt?"

"Some," she admitted. "But I try to hold off on calling the nurse as long as I can. I hate the way those drugs leave me woozy."

"I know what you mean," John agreed. "I get these killer headaches. I put off taking the medicine as long as I can because I hate the feeling it gives me, as though I can't put two thoughts together."

"Like my head is stuffed with cotton," she agreed.

"Right. But the longer I wait, the more medicine I have to take to make it go away. When my wife was alive, she used to make me take the pills immediately. She said she could tell the moment the pain started because I held my head a certain way. I guess she was probably right. But I'm too stubborn to do it by myself."

"What happened to your wife?" Leslie asked, then stopped, worried she might have said something wrong.

But John's tone indicated he accepted it as a natural question, and replied in kind. "She had a weak heart. Always had, ever since she was a kid. The strain of bearing Carmelita was too much for her. We knew about the risk before she became pregnant, but having a child was something she really wanted to do. We prayed about it and decided to accept the risk. She died about two years ago."

"I'm sorry," Leslie said, and felt the truth of the words down deep. "Carmelita is a great kid."

"Yeah, she's a handful." John's strong features melted into a mask of real concern. He looked at her with fathomless dark eyes and said quietly, "I'm really worried about Mama."

"Grace? Why?"

"She's grown so *quiet*."

"I never knew her before," Leslie said slowly, touched by his naked concern. "But she seems okay to me. She's old, and she's had an operation. But she appears to be recovering."

"Physically, maybe. But her spirit's just not there anymore." John lowered his head to inspect the floor at his feet. "She was always so *active*. My dad was the quiet one. I could never faze him. I remember, back when I was still in university, I'd come home all full of excitement and ideas. And worries, a lot of those too. I'd bounce all these things off Pop, and he'd just sit there and listen and nod. Almost never reply. For him, it was enough to see I was taking advantage of a chance he never had. If what I was saying really bothered him, he'd take this attitude like, well, okay, I was young, I'd outgrow these things. Down deep I was still a good boy."

Again there was the sense of her world being jarred by the utterly unexpected. "You went to college?"

"Midwestern."

"What did you study?"

"Engineering."

Leslie's brow furrowed in a concentrated attempt to make sense of what she was hearing. "What are you doing now?"

"Paving stones mostly," John replied distractedly, his mind elsewhere. "Some marble and brickwork, some interior fittings, a little of this and that."

"But why?"

The distress in her voice caused him to lift his head. "I never really thought of doing anything else," he replied simply. "It was what Pop got us into."

"What about leading your own life," she protested. "What about making the most of yourself?"

John shrugged. "I hate offices, and I hate ties. I love being outdoors working with the crews. I love working with my hands. I have all the money I need and I have time to be with my daughter. That seems like a pretty good life to me. How many people do you know can say they are doing work they love?"

Leslie lay back on her pillow, defeated. "Anyway, you were saying about your father."

"Right. Pop was the unshakable rock when I was growing up. He never spoke unless he had something important to say, and then said it with as few words as possible. Mama was exactly the opposite. She always had something to say about everything. That's why it was fun to talk with her. I remember once watching her argue with a telephone book." John showed a smile at the memory. "I used to laugh about it, you know, how this lady who barely finished grade school loved arguing with her college boy. Then I'd get back on the road and be shocked to the core by how much sense she made. Of course, I'd never let her know that."

"Of course," Leslie said quietly.

"My buddies used to love coming home with me. Mama would cook and argue the whole time. We'd sort of roll back to school, too full to walk after a weekend of eating and talking. She's been like that all my life. Nothing made her happier than feeding a houseful of people and arguing with everybody in reach."

His features slipped back into shadows of concern. "Now she's different," he said faintly. "Ever since the accident, she's been a changed woman. First she refused to come into the hospital, and her arguments with me became like full-blown wars. We were shouting at each other for the first time since I was a kid. Night and day it was like that."

He rubbed a hard, worried hand down one side of his face. "Then I show up, ready to sling her over my shoulder and carry her down here if I have to, and she's gone all quiet. She agrees to come, as though the three weeks of arguments never happened. And she's been like that ever since. As if I was speaking with a different person." He raised gravely distressed eyes to her own. "Or like she was only half there."

"I don't know what to tell you," Leslie said softly, and found herself aching for this strange man who cared so little for the things that mattered so much to her, and yet who cared so much, and so deeply. "She really seems all right. Maybe with time she'll come around and be her old self again."

"Yeah, I suppose all we can do is wait and hope." He sighed his way to his feet. "Sorry to have bothered you with all this."

"You haven't bothered me at all."

"Tell her I'll stop by later, okay? I've got to go see about a job." He walked to the door, turned, and offered her a small but genuine smile. "By the way, my daughter thinks you're something special. She goes on about you all the time."

Leslie allowed her own smile to slip away with the shutting of the door. She stared at the empty space where John had just been, and wondered at this strange man whose path had crossed her own.

〜

The Gift

Grace shut the door to the shower room with a grateful sigh. She found it remarkable how much she could treasure something so insignificant as a simple moment of privacy. She felt such a sense of vulnerability and exposure here in the hospital. People were constantly manipulating her. Perfect strangers bathed her, adjusted her clothes, felt her body.

At the same time, she felt a growing matter-of-factness about her own state. Gradually she was taking a mental step back from it all, somehow feeling that in truth she was safe, isolated, protected.

Her sense of accomplishment had shrunk to things she had taken for granted all her life. Walking the length of the hall had been her own personal Everest. The first two days she had not been able to do it. The sense of defeat had been almost overwhelming. Then yesterday, when she had finally made it down and back without stopping, she had felt high as a kite from the success.

Today's goal was to raise her leg high

enough to step into the shower, alone and unaided.

She grasped the metal rail, lifted her leg one inch, another, then dropped it back. She was panting hard, and perspiration beaded her forehead. She leaned against the wall and waited for the weakness to subside. One part of her wanted to weep with rage and frustration. Another part, however, granted a peace strong enough for her to see, to *know*, in this hour of fading strength, that everything truly was all right.

That morning, before her Bible study group had arrived, she had experienced another moment of clarity. It had been the same, and yet different, granting her a sense that one impression built upon the other, leading her in gradual stages towards some unspoken truth.

The hospital's early morning noises had drifted through the closed door as Grace finished her spoken prayers and began to meditate on Christ's cross. Peace descended in gentle sweeping layers, silent heralds of what was yet to come. She knew, however, that even to hope was to bar the door to its arrival. The key was to simply open her heart to the peace and the accompanying stillness, and be grateful for whatever the Lord wished to show her.

Suddenly the image of the cross in her mind took on a commanding clarity. It was not that the outside world faded, or even that she grew confused over what went on inside her head and what was external. The picture simply became *clear*. As gently as the descending peace, her internal image shifted, and for the first time she had the sense she was being given a vision, one which in truth did not come from herself. Not only was she struck by the vividness of what she saw; now she was being *shown*.

She stood at the very foot of the cross. The wood before her eyes was hewn by rough, impatient strokes of a hand-held blade. Her two hands were held outstretched and open-palmed, as though in supplication. They almost but not quite touched the wood.

Suddenly a crystal clear drop fell upon her left palm. An instant later, a second drop fell upon her right palm, this one ruby red. In a moment of recognition, she realized one was

Christ's tear, the other Christ's blood. And both had been shed for her. As they had been shed for all.

In the brief instant came not only the vision but also understanding. There was not a sense of learning something new, but rather seeing familiar lessons brought home in a different manner, crystallized in a heartbeat. She saw and understood the King of heaven and earth loved her in her fallen, sinful, fearing state. He loved her so much He took on mortal form, in sorrow, in compassion, in a sharing of her mortal woes. He came to live, to weep, to love, to suffer, to die. For her. She stood at the foot of the cross and held in her two hands both the reason for His coming and the gift of His passage. Love without measure. Life without end. For her.

As swiftly as it had appeared, the vision faded. In its final instant she felt the unspoken call rise from her mind and heart:

Come.

∼

The Gift

Grace opened her eyes, took a breath, heaved with all her might, and lifted her leg up and over the shower stall's ledge. With a genuine sense of satisfaction, she pulled in her undamaged leg, reached, and turned on the spigots. She stood in the warm water and revelled in her accomplishment.

She was growing older. The hospital and the gift of peace combined to grant her both a distance and a new perspective on her own life. This experience and the accident itself marked a transition.

She also knew this transition of hers was troubling John enormously. But there was nothing she could do about that, except love him the best she could. Her son would simply have to reach his own understanding of the fact that she was changing.

Grace turned off the water and reached for her towel. This was real life, she realized. Not the charade of chasing after youth. Not the lie that time and events could be frozen at a pleasant point. Real life was *change*. Real life was *growth*. And if she was willing to open her heart to what each day brought, she had no doubt it would all work to the good of the Lord.

When she returned to her room, Grace found Leslie on the phone talking to her mother. As she eased herself into bed, the final salutations were given and the phone returned to its place. Then Leslie turned to her and asked, "How was it?"

"Marvelous," Grace sighed, settling back. "Ecstasy."

"Excuse me for being a little bit jealous. I can't wait until I'm able to wash my hair."

"Maybe the swelling will be down far enough this evening for them to fit the cast," Grace offered.

"I hope so. I feel like I'm covered in a sheet of grime. These bed baths don't leave me feeling very clean."

Grace observed, "I haven't heard you mention your father."

"My father?" Leslie's smile became little

more than a grimace. "That's really funny. I was just thinking about him before I called Mom."

"What is funny about it, dear?"

"Oh, nothing, I guess. I can't help but compare my dad with you. He got to be religious too, see. At least, he claimed he did. Oh, I guess he really was. Only what I saw made me *hate* religion."

"Why is that?"

"He was senior vice-president of a local bank. Around the house, Dad was domineering and dictatorial and a pain to live with. I never did see all that much love between my parents, more like they spent a lot of time going through the motions. The older I got, the less they had in common. Then when I was sixteen, he and my mom divorced."

Grace found herself retreating to the inner invitation of peace. She was being bombarded with Leslie's emotions, a solid torrent of outpoured anger and pent-up frustrations. She knew without understanding why it was important that she needed to be there and offer the only gift she could at that moment, which was nonjudgmental compassion.

"It was strange how Mom took the divorce more or less in stride, while it really ended up being hard on Dad. A couple of months after the divorce was final, he turned to religion. It got really hard to be around him after that. I mean, it was hard before, but after that it got *really* hard."

Grace sensed a door appearing before her, an opening in Leslie's shield. The juncture of realization came with a sense of things drawing together, of events past and present joining and melding, of a crossroads appearing. A choice that was wholly Leslie's, and yet one that Leslie could neither see nor understand. It was up to her to point the way. She said gently, "Why do you say that, dear?"

"Once he started his religion kick, he had this thing, whenever anybody disagreed with him, of saying two things. I could sort of carry this checklist into any argument with him, he was that predictable. The first thing was, I've never met anybody like you, I just don't understand you and I doubt anybody ever could. Like, you know, I'm the total freak, and he has perfect judgment about all things, and because I disagree with him, I'm the one who's out in left field. Then the other thing he always said was, I've talked this over with the Lord, and I've studied the Bible, and I feel utterly at peace with my position."

Leslie paused long enough to take a shaky breath. "Listen to me. He's been dead almost ten years now and I'm still mad at him and his religion. Oh, I had all these arguments I came up with at the time, but I never could say them. I don't know why, maybe I should have. Maybe not, though, they probably wouldn't have done any good. I mean, whole nations have gone to war absolutely certain God was on their side, right? How many atrocities have been committed by mankind over the centuries by people who claimed to be led by God?"

"Numbers beyond count," Grace said quietly.

"Right. So here's my dad, absolutely certain there's no need to listen to my side, because he's got God in his corner, and God says whatever my dad happens to feel at that moment is just fine and dandy." Leslie swiped at one cheek. "Look at me. I'm so worked up I could chew nails."

"Perfectly understandable," Grace murmured, more an invitation for her to continue than real words.

"It's always been hard for me to be around people who act like they've got a handle on religion. I know I shouldn't say that to you, but it's true. I mean, so many religious types, they're the absolute worst for refusing to see anything but their own side of an argument, aren't they?"

"So now whenever somebody professes faith in Christ," Grace said softly, "automatically you see falseness and conflict."

Leslie nodded. "Absolutely."

"The sins of your father are a barrier which keep you from seeing the truth of salvation," Grace offered, knowing the time had come to speak. "It is sad but true that many believers use their faith as an excuse to never look within. They have some pain, some hardship that forces them to accept that life as they know it is empty and undirected. So they accept Christ, and that is the last time they ever venture into the tumult of their own mind."

Leslie turned towards Grace, as though truly focusing on her for the very first time.

Grace tried hard to show Leslie real affection in her eyes and voice as she went on, "I see it all the time, I am sorry to say. There are believers, ardent followers of Christ, who claim the presence of darkness every time life and other people do not behave in the manner that these people expect. They refuse to ever look inside themselves, because they are *afraid*. They are *terrified* of facing up to all the things inside themselves that do not measure up to their own self-image. They classify everything uncomfortable or disagreeable they observe in other believers as being sinful or wrong or tainted. They do not think of themselves as being judgmental. They think of it as protecting the faith. While in truth they are protecting their *image* of faith, and their *image* of themselves as believers."

Leslie opened her mouth, then closed it

again. When Grace was sure Leslie was not going to speak, she continued, "Your father saw himself as a businessman and a man of faith. In many respects, he probably was. But at the same time there were innumerable aspects of his personality that were exactly the opposite. This is true with all of us, Leslie. In the Bible it is called the flesh, the old nature, and dates back to the original fall of man.

"But while salvation is given to each and every believer in Christ, a guaranteed gift, there is also the *invitation* from Christ to let His life in us move us toward *being* like Him. We are given grace, you see, but we are *asked* to serve. We are *asked* to improve, to become better lovers and givers and healers. We are *asked* to pray without ceasing. But this can only come through facing up to what is inside ourselves. And this step many people absolutely refuse to take. So they remain spiritually crippled, incapable of the growth *asked* of them."

Grace leaned towards the other bed, as far as her hip would allow, and went on, "But this does not change the truth of God's teachings, my dear. You must believe this. Your immortal soul depends upon accepting the genuineness of my words. Christ is more than any human. He is Lord Almighty, come to earth to grant us what we in our weaknesses and our failings could never earn for ourselves. He is the Way, the path to eternal life. We are mere servants of the perfect Master. You need to find Him for yourself, come to know Him for who He is, in order to understand the truth of my words."

GRACE RESTED and prayed and granted Leslie much-needed space. Grace felt depleted by the strain of their conversation, yet enriched at the same time. She lay with her eyes closed, gave thanks for the gift of being used to convey truth, and prayed for Leslie. Then she began her time of quiet.

Grace had never known such ease in the movement from her prayer of words to her exercise of listening. The peace had never felt so natural. She lay and felt the emotion-charged room fade into the distance.

Again the mental pictures sharpened into an image granted to her from beyond. No longer did she look at the cross. This time she was somehow upon it. There was a moment of panic, of pulling away, yet the gentle Spirit of peace comforted her and offered her the chance to remain and learn from the unexpected.

The fear and the offer and the decision to remain lasted but a mere moment, the chance to see from this perspective a mere moment more. Yet a multitude of lessons were granted in this brief instant. She saw things she had read about and prayed over and dwelled upon most of her life. She watched as they were brought together, not necessarily into a better focus but certainly a different one. She saw from a perspective *beyond* words.

She saw the requirement of dying to the sins of the old self was a step she would take over and over and over, yet each time the step was made fresh and new by the Master's gift. She saw He had taken her pain and her sin and her suffering upon Himself. She saw this was the eternal gift of the Crucifixion, freedom from sins she recognized and those to which she remained blind, from pains and memories and tainted motives and all the things in her life that were polluted by this world. This was Christ's gift of release, by accepting the humiliation and the pain and the filth of fallen man upon His own perfect brow, thus was she saved from the eternal misery of her own failures and sins.

Here He was, ever ready to accept her own human frailties, and her own continued sins, and her ever present fears, all upon himself. Done in utter, perfect, eternal love. Done for her. For her. For her.

She sighed and took a slow breath. Her heart and chest was too full of peace to breathe very deeply. She opened her eyes to a final realization, that change would ever require from her the small death of letting go.

There in the final moment, before the room returned to full focus, came the silently whispered invitation to her mind and heart:

Come.

Later that evening, Carmelita arrived with her father. "Sorry to have brought her a second time," John said, not to Grace but to Leslie. "We're on our own tonight."

"It's fine," she said, and appeared to genuinely mean it.

Carmelita proceeded to hug her grandmother, then to everyone's astonishment turned and hugged Leslie too. Grace drew the little girl back and engaged her and John in conversation long enough for Leslie to collect herself.

After Carmelita's first breathless rush of telling her grandmother all that the afternoon had contained, there was a moment's pause, as though the room held its breath. Then with the quiet calm of ignorance, Leslie said, "Could I ask you something?"

"Anything," Grace said, stroking her granddaughter's hair.

"How is it that you and your son speak English with no trace of any Spanish accent whatsoever? I mean, I realize you are Americans, but still with most Hispanics I meet I can hear a hint of accent. But with you two, if I closed my eyes I truly could not say where you were from."

John was already on his feet before she had

finished speaking. "It's getting late."

"I can tell her," Carmelita announced.

"We need to let Mama have her rest," John said, his tone stiff.

"I've said something wrong," Leslie said worriedly. "Please excuse me."

Grace found herself suddenly occupied with an internal tolling, a resounding force that echoed about her mind and heart. "It's all right," she said, to her son as well as to Leslie. And somehow, even with the realization of what needed to be done, she knew it truly was. "There is no harm whatsoever in an honest question."

"'Life certainly is a strange place to call home'," Carmelita chanted. "That was what Mama Johnson used to say all the time, right, gramma?"

"That's exactly right, child," Grace said softly, nodding her reassurance to John. Her son stood awkwardly at the foot of the bed, unsure of what to do or say.

Carmelita giggled. "I know that story."

"Not all of it, you don't," Grace replied. Again the peaceful force filled her, leaving no room for doubt, nor place for the customary terrors that normally trapped her whenever the memories threatened to surface.

The little girl's dark head popped up. "Why don't I?"

"Because it is not a pretty story," Grace replied. "And such stories need to wait until you are bigger."

Lita stood and placed both hands on her hips. "I am so a big girl. And I want to know the story."

"Soon," Grace said, watching the emotions flicker across her son's features like the passage of a summer storm. Yes, soon she would share the tale with both her son and her granddaughter. But not now. This evening she would return Leslie's gift of honesty with one of her own. She turned to Leslie and explained, "From the age of three I was raised by a family called Johnson."

"I know, I know," Lita chimed in breathlessly. "They ran a hardware store in Iowa. They didn't speak any Spanish, and so you spoke only English and forgot everything you knew. They named you Grace, because you didn't ever tell them your own name, and you said 'gracias' to them every time they came around you. Then when you grew up and met Grandaddy you were very ashamed when he spoke to you in Spanish and you didn't know what to say except 'si'." The little girl had a giggle like tiny silver bells. "And Grandaddy thought that was very funny, since he had asked you for directions to the train station."

"It was the only time in my life I wished I knew my mother tongue," Grace agreed, feeling the pressure mount in her chest. It was indeed time. "When we started courting, I began Spanish lessons."

"It really is late," John said quietly. "I have to start at five tomorrow. Say good-bye, Lita."

"Awww." Carmelita spun and hugged her grandmother, then turned to the other bed and said, "Good night, pretty lady."

"You can call me Leslie," she replied, accepting the hug with tightly closed eyes. Her tone suggested she was still sorry over what she had said. "Would you like to take some more flowers?"

"Ohhh, can I?"

"Absolutely," she said, releasing the little girl only reluctantly. "I have far too many."

"How can somebody have too many flowers?" Carmelita danced over, tucked her hands up to her chin in indecision, then stood on tiptoe and said, "Can I have some of the pretty yellow and pink ones?"

"They are called lilies," Grace said.

"Lilies," Carmelita repeated. "They're beautiful."

"Take them all," Leslie said. "I would like you to have them."

Carmelita looked a plea at her father, who said to Leslie, "I have never met anyone who loved flowers as much as she does. Thank you."

"Mommy did," Carmelita said. "She used to have a garden. I know 'cause Daddy told me. I was real little then and I forgot, but he remembers for me."

"You're welcome," Leslie said quietly.

"Mommy's with God," Carmelita announced, her eyes still on the flowers and unable to see the effect her words were having on the adults. "She was very tired after she had me. God kept her here for as long as He could, though. Right, Daddy?"

"That's exactly right," John said, gazing on his daughter, his voice a soft rumble.

"But then He decided Mommy needed to rest up in heaven where the angels could look after her." Carmelita turned back around and said to Leslie, "Sometimes I talk to Mommy when I say my prayers. I'm going to tell her about you tonight. She'll like you."

John picked up the big vase with the lilies. For the first time since Leslie had asked her question, he met her eyes. The depths to his dark gaze left Grace having difficulty swallowing. But all he said was, "I'll tell the nurse we'll bring her vase back tomorrow. Good night. Sleep well."

When the door had sighed shut, Leslie said, "I'm really sorry, I didn't mean to offend anyone."

"You didn't," Grace replied. "It wasn't what you said at all."

Leslie motioned towards the empty space at

the foot of their beds. "But John—"

"I unfortunately insist on keeping hold to a vast collection of fears and painful memories," Grace said. "Some of them have infected my son, often without him knowing why."

"I'm not sure I understand."

"I don't know when I was born, or where," Grace replied. "When I was a young girl, Mother Johnson chose the twenty-fifth of June as my birthday, because she knew how much I loved parties and presents, and it was as far away from Christmas as we could get."

"I really didn't mean to pry," Leslie said.

Grace turned her head on the pillow. "You were kind enough to share from the heart with me this afternoon. I would like to repay your gift with a story of my own. It is one I have not spoken of in years, and I think I have carried it long enough. Would you mind if I burdened you with it?"

"It wouldn't be a burden," Leslie said awkwardly.

"Don't say that too quickly." Grace turned her eyes towards the ceiling. "My husband once told me it was the elder's responsibility to keep the past alive."

"Elder of what?"

"Tribe, nation, family, church, whatever. Enrico said most people make the mistake of sweetening the past, granting it promise the future could never fulfill. Children especially needed to know the good with the bad, he said. How else were they to prepare themselves, since the future was nothing but the next layer to be set upon the past."

There was a moment's silence, then Leslie said, "I've never thought of it like that."

But Grace was too caught up with her own past to notice that once again she had managed to shake the young woman's world. "This particular memory has not been spoken of since the early days of my own marriage. Strange that I would insist on holding on to one that has brought me only terror in the night. But there you are."

Grace paused to shift herself, the pressure of what needed to come out making her entire body uncomfortable. "I really do not remember much of my early childhood. There are brief flashes, but since most of them have become associated with nightmares, I try to refuse them. I try to see my life beginning with the days in the Iowa hardware store. But they did not. And I see I have made a mistake in lying to myself in this way."

"Maybe it wasn't a lie," Leslie said quietly. "Maybe you just weren't ready to face that particular truth before."

The accuracy of her words resounded deep within Grace. She turned to look in the young woman's direction. "Thank you, my dear."

"For what?"

"For caring." She turned her gaze back toward the ceiling, willing herself onwards before her courage failed. "I remember dusty streets, and walking them without shoes. I remember a hot sun, much hotter than here. I remember rows and rows of wooden shacks. I remember, I remember . . ."

The pressure mounted. There was a burning sense of upward urgency, like a bubble of intensely hot air rising towards the surface, released now, demanding to be set free. "I remember," she said again, her voice throaty. "I remember that my mother worked in tall green fields. I remember that she left before the sun was hot, and came back as the day was cooling. I remember she was very tired almost all the time. I remember an old woman looked after me and several other young children by tying a rope around our waist, and sitting under a tree, and watching us squeal and play in the dusty earth.

"I remember that my mother became sick," Grace went on, and realized with a tiny detached portion of her mind that the faintest hint of a Spanish accent was creeping into her voice. But the pressure of release was too strong for her to pay it very much mind for very long. "I remember that many others became sick as well, and then the old woman who watched us died. I remember that very clearly now, turning to her one afternoon, and realizing she was no longer there, and wondering how that could be, because her body was there, but the old woman was not. It was the first time I had ever seen death, and I remember it very clearly."

The room was so still Grace could very well have been alone. But somehow she knew Leslie was listening, helping her to ease this burden from her heart by offering the gift of silent caring. It gave her the strength to go on, on towards the final release. "I remember that afternoon, because no one came to feed me, and all the other children had disappeared. One by one they simply were not there any more. And the shacks, which had always been quiet, became quieter still. Before it was the quietness of very tired people going about their lives. Now it was the quietness of no life at all. The air hung very heavy, and it stank very bad. I remember crying, but not much, because somehow I knew there was nobody there to hear me.

"After the old woman died, I managed to free myself from the rope and crawl to the little shack that was my home. My mother was there, I remember, and she was awake and looking straight at me, but she did not seem to understand I was hungry. She was crying. I remember looking at her face and seeing the tears and wanting her to get up and fix me something to eat because I was very hungry.

"Then the men came. I remember being very scared, even after they picked me up and fed me something. I remember they wore boots, and there were not many people in my little world who had leather shoes, and they scraped across my floor with loud noises which did not belong. I remember screaming when they picked up my mother and carried her out to a truck. I remember how they picked me up and took me outside and put me into the truck beside my mother, but still I was scared, because the truck was very loud and it smelled bad. But what smelled worse were all the people who they loaded in around my mother. All the people of my world were suddenly nothing more than weak sacks of flesh and bone, who were lifted in by people wearing boots and gloves and white masks. Strange that I would remember the masks, but I can see them now, and how a few of them without masks wore kerchiefs knotted up around their noses and faces, and held them tight against their chins when their hands were free."

Grace realized she was crying, but could not spare even a moment to wipe away the tears. "I remember they drove us in the hot sun for the longest while. The truck was open and flat and full to the brim with silent, stinking bodies. They took us to a city, the first city I had ever seen. They drove us to a big red brick building, where other people with masks came out and started unloading all the bodies. I remember how these people wore white, and how the inside of the building smelled different than anything I had ever smelled in my entire life. They were sharp smells, unfriendly smells, that bit at my nose and throat as I cried for my mother. But they did not let me stay with her. They spoke in a language I did not understand, and took her away on a white bed which rolled down a long corridor under bright white lights. And other people held me while I screamed, and they touched me with their rubber gloves and looked at me over their white masks."

The burning release left a great gaping hole in her heart, a searing emptiness which she knew even in her moment of agony was good.

Was right. She paused to take a few ragged breaths and swallow several times and wipe her face, and then continued, "I don't know how long I stayed there in the hospital. Time did not seem to matter there in that world of false white lights which had taken me from my mother. Then one day a couple came in to the room where I was kept. They were white people, and they spoke that same language which I did not understand. I remember the woman wore a dark blue dress, and had a pretty gold cross on a chain around her neck, and the man had another cross on his lapel. I remember that they both looked down at me with such love that suddenly I knew everything was going to be all right. Strange I would know this when I had never seen them before, and could not understand a word they were saying. But I knew. I remember that I started to cry again, this time because somebody was there who cared about everything that was inside of me, and I remember lifting up my hands to the woman, and suddenly she was crying too, and the man had tears in his eyes, and the woman picked me up, and the man put his arms around both of us. And then they took me home."

Grace was quiet for a time, breathing deeply, taking stock of the changes within herself, the new vistas appearing now that the barriers were down. Then she realized Leslie was still there, still waiting, still a part of her story. And she found herself too ashamed to even look in Leslie's direction. "I am very tired, dear," Grace said shakily. "I think perhaps I should get some sleep."

Then the figure in the next bed stirred and asked quietly, "Would you like me to read you another Bible passage?"

And with the young woman's words came a sense of overwhelming rightness. Grace smiled towards the ceiling and said, "I think that would be wonderful."

That night the awning hoists outside the window banged against the metal railings in the wind. Trolleys squeaked up and down the passage. Grace's breath came and went in soft regular sighs. Little sounds filled Leslie's dark room with reminders of how trapped she was. Things that were always there, always covered by the hectic nature of her life, now lay revealed.

Being normally so independent, the feeling of utter dependence was hard on Leslie. Usually in her life, when she wanted to do something, she did so. Now the will was still there, but the physical ability was not. The smallest thing, the tiniest action, meant enduring more pain.

Not only had she lost her sense of self-reliance, now she also had to ask someone else for help. It was so difficult to ask. She found herself almost tearfully grateful if the nurse offered to do something, rather than forcing her to ask and thus humble herself.

There in the darkness, with freedom only to be found in her heart and mind, she glimpsed her barrier of pride. Accepting God meant *asking*. Admitting she was powerless and asking for help. Asking for forgiveness. Receiving love.

The series of blinding glimpses continued to illuminate her night. She recalled the moment of her accident. In the space of one heartbeat, her whole impression of who she was had been stripped away. She had never realized how much she had taken for granted her independence and her power and her own self-image. Now she was trapped, held in place, and forced to look at herself. See beyond the facade she presented to the world. See beyond the carefully erected barriers and half-truths and things she tried so hard to make true.

She realized that one effect of the accident was to begin separating her sense of identity from her body. This body needed to be checked and bandaged and bathed. This body was intimately connected to her, yet she was discovering herself to be more than just flesh and bone and clothes and job and title and responsibilities and possessions.

In those lonely hours, Leslie found herself coming to realize the genuine person was internal. And with this came a question echoing about the darkness: Who was she really?

She was struck with a sense of absolute certainty she had been moving toward this moment for a very long time. Strange how that comforted her, to know in some mysterious yet solid way that all of these events had a purpose. Some invisible Presence was there, actively guiding, granting meaning to both her accident and her fears.

There in the darkness, isolated from all that had defined her world, she felt a need growing from within the emptiness she had strived so hard to ignore. She found thoughts coalescing, rising from some deep recess within her, a prayer so soft as almost to be beyond her conscious ability to know what it contained, yet so strong that she was lifted along with the words. Wafted up, up, higher and higher until she was no longer bound by either the hospital or the night. Lifted beyond all that she knew as real, into a realm of peace and comfort and illumination so strong she did not even need her earthly eyes to see.

To *see*.

∾

Saturday morning John stopped by after his usual hours of weekend work to find Leslie alone and sitting up in bed and smiling. "Your timing is perfect. Grace left for her bath about fifteen minutes ago."

He stepped in and let the door close behind him. "You are looking great," he said, and meant it.

She beamed. "I washed my hair today," she said. "You can't imagine how much it means to be clean again."

John looked down at his own sweaty clothes, suddenly ashamed of how he must look. "Yes, I can." And then it hit him, how the last time he had felt shame over his appearance was before his wife had become ill.

"Come sit down," Leslie said. "I have something I need to tell you."

Still a little shaken, John drew a chair up close to her bed. When he was settled, Leslie went on, "I've been giving a lot of thought to your concerns about Grace, and I have to tell you I am ninety-nine percent positive she is fine. Really and truly doing well."

The simple warmth and confidence in her voice left him with a burning sensation behind his eyes. "I've been so worried," he managed. "The doctor said she was growing too quiet."

"I didn't know her before," Leslie said, clearly wanting to offer him not only reassurance, but honest comfort. "But I have been spending a lot of time with her, not just laying beside her but talking with her." The young woman hesitated, and a look of shy joy passed over her features, "And learning from her. I really think she is fine."

"But she's so different," John said, allowing his worries to surface. "So much quieter and more distant."

Leslie leaned towards him, and said in a voice more gentle than he would have thought possible. "Maybe she's growing old, John. Have you ever thought of that?"

The burning sensation returned. "All the time."

"I have been thinking a lot about that too. There isn't much else to do here but think." A flicker of shadows passed over her, like clouds over a sunlit field. "I used to think I had to hold onto my youth and my energy and my beauty and all my strength, because when I lost it I lost everything. But I've been listening and watching and talking now with your mother for a week, and I have learned she is one of the most beautiful women I have ever met. And part of her beauty is the fact that she is still learning and growing. And for her, part of this learning and growing just now is the need to accept the fact that she is growing old."

John nodded his head slowly, amazed at how deeply this woman's words resounded within him. "That makes a lot of sense."

"I really don't think you need to worry any more," Leslie said, the light and gentleness returning. "She is going to be just fine."

"You don't know how much it means to hear this," John said, his relief a wave which crested and broke and flooded his being.

"You are a very good man," Leslie said, her eyes shining. "In a way, hard as it is for me to say this, I'm glad I had to come here. It's given me the chance to see beyond what I always thought was so important in people. I can only hope I can carry these lessons with me when I leave."

The quiet fervor in her voice carried him to his feet. "Have they told you when you're going to be released?"

"Tomorrow, same as your mother."

He took great pains in turning and lifting the chair with both hands, settling it precisely back against the wall, looking anywhere but at her as he asked, "Do you think you might like to go out sometime, maybe have dinner, see a movie or something?"

Her silence finally caused him to turn around. It was only when he stood vulnerable and exposed and held within her brilliant gaze that she replied, "I think that would be wonderful."

Grace was scarcely back inside the room when Leslie announced, "Your son has asked me out on a date."

One hand clutched at Grace's chest while the other sought the railing at the foot of her bed. "You can't do that to an old woman," she scolded, forcing her legs to carry her around and onto the bed.

"What's the matter? I thought you'd be pleased."

"My dear, you can't imagine how good this news is. I've been after him since the year after his wife died, trying to get him to break through his cocoon and get out there and meet people."

Her voice tinted with astonishment, Leslie said, "He hasn't had a date in two years?"

"If he has, John certainly has not told me about it. Or Carmelita." Grace did her best to hide the swell of emotion by fiddling with her sheet. "He's lost himself in his work, he's lost himself in Carmelita, and he's spent far too much time with me. Oh, I'm blessed beyond measure to have him as a son. But I have ached for him and his loneliness. A young child and an old woman and work are no way to fill that empty hole."

"I've had a tough time learning that myself,"

Leslie said slowly. "And I didn't even have the child or mother. I've let work pretty much consume me." She looked over at the other bed. "There's so much I want to take out of here with me, and that's one of the lessons I hope I'll never forget. I don't know what I'm going to do once I get back, but I know there are going to be some changes. Big ones."

Grace felt such a pride and a love for the young woman next to her that it took her a few moments before she could say, "My, how you've grown."

"I'll say." Leslie positively shone in her smile. "Thanks to you and this chance to get away from the pressures of work for a while. I never realized how much I've been using it as a block to seeing what life really is and who I really am."

"Hold on to this," Grace urged. "Don't let it go once you're back out there and your old life starts pulling at you."

"I want to," Leslie said determinedly. "I really do. I worry about that, though."

"Ask the Lord above for help," Grace replied. "And seek the comfort of other believers."

The power of what she said struck the two of them simultaneously. *Other* believers. Grace saw the sensations sweep across Leslie's fresh-scrubbed face, and felt another tug of love and concern for the young woman fill her own heart. "It's easier than you think to lose yourself out there. I've watched it happen with John. After his wife died, he threw himself into his company with both hands and both feet. His pain has long since gone, but still he holds to the old habits of working until he's almost ready to drop. I don't know what would have happened if Carmelita had not been there. But she is not enough of a reason to have him slow down as much as he should."

But something in what she had said had hit Leslie a solid hammer-blow. "John has a company?"

"It was his father's and now it is his," Grace said distractedly, still caught in her worries for her son. "It's like any company, I suppose. It will take as much as any person has to give and still want more. And the problems the economy has been going through for the past couple of years has been a perfect reason for him not to slow down. But he needs to. He really does."

"How large a company?" Leslie asked.

Grace looked over at the other bed. "I've told you all this."

"I don't think so."

"But I must have."

"I think I would have remembered something like that, but who knows with all these drugs," Leslie said, her voice a little shaky. "What do they do?"

"Paving stones," Grace said distractedly. "I know I've told you this. Enrico started us in that. Now John does a lot of things. Marble interiors and exteriors, external tiles, a little specialized paving."

"Is this still a family-owned concern?"

"Of course."

"How many employees do you have?"

Something in her tone finally worked its way through to capture Grace's attention. "It was up to one hundred and forty," she replied, turning to look straight at Leslie. "But with the recession we had to pare down. We let thirty people go. That was very hard for us. But we managed to make sure everyone we laid off found other work. And twelve of those have been rehired." A hint of very real pride shone in her voice. "You can't imagine what it means to be able to call someone and ask if they'd like to come back, and hear them shout with joy."

"No," Leslie agreed, her voice suddenly very small. "I can't."

"We try to be good to our employees. But still, we're running a business, and you know what that means."

"I know," Leslie said softly.

"Especially in such hard times. Everybody is pushed to their limit, and sometimes not even that is good enough. Tempers are short, and, well, a boss has to be a boss. Otherwise there would not be a company there to run." Grace watched the effect her words were having on Leslie, and found her own concerns pushed to one side. The young woman seemed to be sink- ing down inside herself. Grace continued, "We try to treat everyone fairly. There are performance evaluations and some promotions every twelve months. We all have the same health care and pension scheme. We try to make them feel appreciated. We have picnics and family days at least once every three months. The office is part of the factory, so they can come and see John or any of the other managers whenever they want. And John spends the better part of every day working at one site or another."

Grace paused, wondering what it was she had said, and what she should say next. "But you know how people complain, especially when they're tired and life seems a little out of their control. So we don't often have any idea how our people really feel about us. Then to hear them shout for joy when we call, and jabber their thanks when we ask them back," Grace smiled at the memory. "It makes us feel good."

"And they all have returned?"

"Everybody we've asked back so far."

"You must be paying quite a bit above the market norm."

"No, salaries in the paving and stonework industries are fairly standardized." She peered at the other bed. "Why do you ask?"

"No reason, I suppose," Leslie said, settling deeper into her pillow. "It just surprises me a little to hear that your son runs his own company."

"Or that it runs him," Grace said, returning to her own worries. "He hates the office, and doesn't spend enough time seeing to all the things that need doing. I've been helping out, watching over the staff and checking the books and seeing to a lot of the bills and bidding. But while I've been here I've come to realize I need to slow down. I really have to."

Then it struck her, a thought with such blinding force that it left her stunned. She remained silent, struggling to bring it all into focus, until she realized the moment was slipping away. She said as casually as she could muster, "You know what he really needs is a good executive. Somebody he can truly call his own right hand. Someone he can give all the office responsibilities to. Someone who would free him once and for all to do what he loves and is best at, working on the jobs."

When no reply was forthcoming, Grace turned her head a tiny fraction, far enough to look over and see Leslie laying there, staring at the ceiling with a stunned expression of her own. Grace turned back around, and closed her eyes with a vastly contented sigh.

Sunday morning was a happy-sad time for Leslie. She shared in the delighted laughter of being truly well enough to enjoy being released, and yet her humor was touched by faint brushstrokes of sorrow. Whatever happened next, no matter how ready she was to leave the hospital behind, Leslie knew something beautiful was coming to an end.

Leslie shut her case, stood, examined herself in the mirror, and faltered. There was so much of the old Leslie there, staring back at her, challenging the depth and the solidity of everything she had learned. She found herself facing the moment of walking out that door with very real fear.

She sighed, shut her closet, and turned to find Grace watching her. The older lady was seated upon the edge of her bed, her satchel at her feet. She was dressed in a fetching suit of grey-blue flannel, a single strand of pearls laced about her neck. Her leather-bound diary rested in her lap. A pen was held poised in one hand. Leslie asked, "What are you writing?"

"A verse from Mother Johnson's favorite hymn," Grace replied. "I feel as though the words have taken on new light while I've been in here." She looked down and read softly,

> When I survey the wondrous cross,
> On which the Prince of glory died,
> My richest gain I count but loss,
> And pour contempt on all my pride.

"That's beautiful," Leslie said.

"Yes it is." She closed the little book, inspected Leslie's face, and said, "You're scared, aren't you, dear."

Leslie swallowed and managed a nod.

Grace patted the bed beside her. "Come sit down."

Leslie reached for the crutches propped beside the closet and put them under her arms. "Guess I'd better start getting used to them." Although she was fitted with a walking cast, the doctor had urged her to use the crutches whenever her ankle began to complain. All the standing and packing and preparing had left it a little sore. Leslie maneuvered herself around the bed, and settled down beside the older lady. "There."

Grace settled a hand upon her knee. "I leave here having gained a new daughter. I want you to remember that, and know you are always welcome in my home. Always."

She looked into Grace's face, was met with concern and love. "I can't thank you enough for everything you've done."

"I could think of nothing that would make me happier," Grace replied, "than having you pray with me."

Leslie gave a tiny nod, then asked in a voice scarcely above a whisper, "Would you say the words?"

She closed her eyes and held Grace's hands. Her heart filled with a sense of reassuring peace, a gift which was both hers to have and hers to give. She listened to Grace's prayer, but in truth what she heard was the comforting knowledge that this peace was hers to keep, a gift which would be with her always.

They had scarcely finished when the door exploded back, making them both start. Carmelita flew into the room, her little eyes filled with indescribable excitement. "Guess what! Daddy's got on a *tie*!"

Then the little girl truly saw Leslie, and she gasped, "You're beautiful!"

Grace chided gently, "You've grown too big to give your grandmother a hug?"

Carmelita raced over, hugged each woman in turn. "Daddy's down talking to the nurses and signing stuff. He said to come down and see if you're ready." She fingered Leslie's brilliant white blouse. "Is this real silk?"

"Yes,"

"Wow." Her attention shifted to the rust-colored skirt. "This is nice too. What is it called?"

"Cotton suede," Leslie said.

"You have really nice clothes." Carmelita's

bright gaze shifted upwards. "And your hair looks nice too. Did you dress up for Daddy?"

Leslie started to shy away from the child's directness, then decided she should meet it head on. "I certainly did."

"You're beautiful. He'll like that." She giggled into her hand. "He wouldn't tell me, but I think he dressed up for you too. Do you like my daddy?"

"Very much," Leslie said, feeling warmth flood her as Grace squeezed her hand.

"He likes you too. He talked about you last night. He asked me if I really liked you or if I was just talking about you." Her dark eyes shone with the joy of a shared secret. "Know what I told him?"

Leslie found herself too concerned with this little girl's opinion to even speak, so made do with a shade of a nod.

"I said you were the nicest person I've met in a whole long while. Nicer even than my teacher Miss Carroll." She cocked her head to one side. "I said I really really liked you a lot. A lot a lot a lot."

The Gift

"Thank you," Leslie managed softly.

The door sighed open, and a very sheepish John entered. He wore a charcoal grey sports coat, black flannel slacks, a white shirt with dark grey stripes, and a matching grey tie.

His daughter announced, "They're ready, Daddy."

"So I see." His hair was cut and brushed, his face was bronzed, his bearing very erect. "Good morning, ladies."

"Hello, John," Grace said quietly. Something in her voice caused Leslie to turn her way. She was surprised to find the older lady's eyes were glistening.

"You look very nice," John said. "Both of you."

"So do you," Leslie replied, thinking he was one of the most handsome men she had ever seen.

A flicker of nervous tension creased his features. John gestured towards the door and said stiffly, "Mama, the nurse said you might want to use one of their wheelchairs for a couple of days. I told her I'd ask, is all."

The room held its breath. Even Carmelita turned solemn. Grace nodded slowly, then said, "I think that might be a very good idea."

John could not help but gape. "You do?"

"There is no need to overtire myself and slow the healing process," Grace replied loftily. "This way I can walk only so much as I feel is right."

Leslie beamed up at him, and said, "Everything is going to be okay, John."

He looked from one woman to the other, then touched the knot of his tie and said nervously, "I was planning to take Lita and Mama to church. I would be honored if you would join us."

"There is nothing," Leslie replied, meeting his gaze as openly as she knew how, "that I would like more."

Grace allowed herself to be wheeled down the hallway, smiled her good-byes at the nurse's station, and knew she was leaving more than just the hospital behind. The memories she carried with her still, yet the fears would no longer whisper their terrors into her night.

Some of her strength and her vitality was being left behind as well, and this was hard for her. But she was cushioned by the peace that filled her, and by the feeling that she was going in the direction chosen both by her and for her. That her life's course continued upon a solid path, that her aging was a natural part of existence, that her embracing it was an important step in her own continued growth.

The peace that enveloped her cushioned the power of these understandings, and helped her welcome the unknowns that lay beyond the hospital doors. The home and the routines that awaited her would both be what she had left, and something new entirely. Her world would be gradually adjusted to fit the new person she was becoming. And knowing she was not alone granted her the strength to accept this with calmness.

Her morning prayer time had known a moment of that clarity again, a final gift before this embarking upon a new stage in life's road. This time, the vision had sharpened in its very first instant, again taking her in an unexpected direction. In the instant of its coming, Grace understood these moments were not what she should ever seek, for they in themselves were mere sensations. What she should continually strive for was to move ever closer to that which lay *beyond* the images.

Once more she saw from the perspective of the cross, yet this time there was no sense of viewing where she was. Instead, she was granted a glimpse of what lay further ahead.

She looked out upon a bridge, one illuminated by a soft inner light. In that brief instant, she realized that the bridge was in truth the risen Christ. It was by His death the bridge was made. And beyond the bridge stood the beckoning fields of Home.

This was His purpose in descending from the throne of heaven—to die for her, to prepare the way for her. The eternal Home awaited her arrival. No matter how long she remained upon this earth, she knew, no matter when her body might finally sigh its last, still would He be there and waiting to bring her Home. Christ's call was a call not to death on a cross, but to go with Him *beyond* the cross, to pass over the bridge of His making and enter life everlasting.

As they approached the hospital's outer doors, Grace decided her first act upon arriving home would be to write in the back of her leather diary another Bible passage. The words would remain for her the greatest gift of this time, the lesson that bound all the other gifts together. They came from the fourteenth chapter of John, and read, "Peace I leave with you; my peace I give unto you. Do not let your hearts be troubled and do not be afraid."

Grace smiled and bid the nurse farewell, took her first breath of freedom, and heard once more the silent clarion call to her heart:

Come.